Super Holly Hansson in:
Super Bad Hair Day!

DAVE M. STROM

ISBN-10 1535481587:
ISBN-13: 978-1535481588

CONTENTS

ACKNOWLEDGMENTS

Thanks to Batton Lash (no relation to my barber), for your cover art and for helping me design Super Holly's costume; to Anya Kagen, for your editing that made me brutally rewrite; and to Anne James, for your editing comments that finally convinced me that my stories were good enough to publish (after another rewrite). ·

And thanks to my barber Lash for keeping my hair nice even when I get cranky, to Tina Gibson for showing me what karate looks and sounds like without scaring me much, to James Hanna and his open mic for giving me a stage, to the self-publishing geeks at comic book conventions, and to the ladies in my first critique group who started a super romance when they told me that Holly Hansson and Cal Critbert—my Superwoman and my Batman—made a perfect couple.

1 SUPER BAD HAIR DAY!

SURFVILLE, CALIFORNIA. THE BARBERSHOP "LASH'S PLACE." LATE AUGUST. 4:32 P.M.

Wonder Woman never had bad hair days in the comic books.

Super Holly Hansson lived in California. And the blue-supersuited and red-caped medusa in the barbershop wall mirror held her gaze like a starship tractor beam. Blond knots and tangles poked out of her thick asphalt helmet. Holly forced her trembling fists to stay at her sides: if she tore off that icky oobleck, her super-strength would take half her hair with it.

Old fingers slipped over Holly's hand. Her hand that could squash a cannonball like a ripe plum. She unclenched her fist and turned to her barber Lash, she so needed some comforting words. She got some.

"Holly, you look like you got into a fight with a cement mixer and lost!" Lash's hair and mustache were grayer, but his bespectacled eyes were still bright. And fixated on Holly's train wreck of a hairdo.

"What kind of super stuff did you get into?"

"Long story," Holly said, a smile twitching her lips. Same old Lash, he'd said a word other than *stuff*. New road smell tingled her nose. Hers was not a little nose, so it was a lot of tingle. And the mirror medusa grabbed her eyes harder, and her telltale-heart thumped her latest deadline into her brain, *he's coming, HE'S COMING,* **HE'S COMING FOR ME!**

Holly swallowed hard and breathed slow. She took her barber's hand in both of hers. "Lash. Can you fix my hair by five?"

Lash's eyes bugged out so far Holly was scared he'd ruin his old cataract surgery. He did an uncanny impression of a cranky old starship doctor: "I'm a barber, not a road repairman!"

"PLEASE?" Oops, Holly had come dangerously close to giving Lash a bloody nose with a spittle bullet. "The scariest of all the supers is coming for me. He's dark, he's grim, there's no escaping him! And I can't face him," Holly had grabbed her head and had to force herself to let go, "like THIS!" She pumped pleading into her eyes and loosened her super-strong tear ducts to let one drop run down her cheek. "Help me, Lash. You're my only hope."

Lash frowned, deepening his few wrinkles. "But... how'm I gonna... you don't get scared, you get mad... you..." He shook his head. "You and your big blue eyes. Lemme think." He scanned dozens of customer photos checkerboarding the walls like spirits of haircuts past. Then he smiled like Lex Luthor putting the last screw into the ray-gun that would shred Superman into sub-atomic particles. "Yeah. That'll do it."

Holly followed his gaze to a photo of a hard hat guy on an oil rig. *What kind of hair-brained plot is he hatching?*

Lash's lips moved as he expertly texted on a smart phone. That was new. Holly remembered Lash's old phone calls: *Holly, can you come in? My frakkin' computer ate up my email again!* He'd used a different word than *frakkin'*. Lash turned to Holly, and despite Holly's super-strength, he pinned her down with a super-tough gaze. "This is a job for my hairdresser."

"But you always do my hair!" Another piece of Holly's past hung over a cliff!

Lash pointed, not to the old shampooing station, but to a chair near a big metal sink. That was new too. "I'll start, Ann will finish, and that's IT! Now have a seat."

"Okay," Holly sighed. She shuffled over and sat. "When did you put in this bathtub?"

Lash fumbled on the shelf above her head. "Few weeks ago. Some of you supers have special hair needs. Heroic Hippie's twenty-foot ponytail takes a quart of shampoo." He pulled out a blow torch. "I use this to style the Human Flame's mohawk." He looked down at her and grinned. "Now tell me about your day, little Miss Storyteller."

That old nickname. So sweet of him, he knew she loved to perform. Holly put on the pompous voice she used when reading her stories at open mics. "Brave and bold Super Holly Hansson, the world's mightiest superhero, received a clarion call that the horrible Harry Headbutt was quarter-mile leaping and bounding toward downtown..."

SEASIDE CITY, CALIFORNIA. 3:37 P.M.

...leaving fear and potholes in his wake! Holly flew through the summer sky, staying just under the speed of sound to avoid getting another sonic-boom speeding ticket. She checked her Wonder-Woman-esque e-bracelet, which she used not to deflect bullets—she was already bulletproof—but to make phone calls and to navigate her flying. Why couldn't her phone's map app project a destination dot on the city streets below? She faced front again, toward danger, toward duty, toward— *SHPLLLPTT!*

Holly sputtered and spat. *Why don't bugs ever splat in Superman's face?* She reached to wipe.

Oops! And lost her aerodynamic pose! City streets, windowy tall buildings, and clear blue sky churned into a 600-mile-per-hour kaleidoscope!

"ULP!" Afternoon iced coffee leaped up her esophagus. She flipped feet forward and dug her heels into the air. It was silly, but she hadn't found a better way to midair stop... stop... STOP!

Her heroic heart hammered as she hovered. A foot from her face stood tall tenth-floor lettering: FIRST COASTAL BANK. She wiped icky insect guts off her face and looked down.

Now THAT was a dot! In the street before the bank, a dozen cops formed a dark blue mound that rippled like a walrus corking a geyser. If Harry was under there, he could mash those cops into dark blue meatballs! A hundred riot-geared police surrounded that mound, along with some abandoned road work, a terrified road crew, and some parked cars. Shops were shut tight. Pedestrians cowered behind the police line. Paparazzi spotted Holly and zoomed their telephoto lenses. Holly longed to zoom her finger.

She landed and stood hand-on-hips heroic. The public liked that. Ugh, her costume had ridden up her butt again. Paparazzi liked that. She reached under her cape and tugged. *Take that, super wedgie!*

She walked up to the police line and put her hand on a cop's shoulder. "I'll take it from here, guys."

The cop looked over *her* shoulder and smirked at Holly. "Give him some girl power!"

"Sorry. And I will." Holly strode toward the mound and yelled a fair warning. "Give it up, butthead! Or get beaten up by a girl! AGAIN!"

From under the heap of police erupted a gorilla growl: "YELLOW HAIR?" The heap shook like a volcano. "HARRY HATE YELLOW HAIR!!!"

All at once! Car alarms blared! Dogs howled! Windows shattered! Windows computers crashed, wait, they always did that. And the mound of cops exploded like...

LASH'S PLACE. 4:42 P.M.

"...ants from a firecrackered anthill... HEY!" Holly wished for an iron bar to chew, like her dentist had recommended instead of grinding her teeth.

She'd stayed quiet when easily distracted Lash had taken two phone calls. She'd growled, "Take it on voicemail," when Lash had almost taken a third. She'd stayed still as Lash had softened the asphalt with the torch and scraped it off with a chisel. But now Holly grabbed the armrest with a ***CREAK*** when Lash had

5

elbowed Holly's chest for the FIFTH TIME! She blurted, "Stop bumping my bumps!

"Sorry, Holly," Lash snapped right back at her, "but I gotta work fast, and some of you is closer to me than used to be!" With a groan, he straightened up, popping vertebrae like knuckles. His eyes lowered to Holly's chest, then to her face. "Can I ask you something?"

Oh, boy, here it comes. When Holly received her superpowers, she had also grown a super-bosom in under two minutes. She wished he'd kid her about her beaky nose again. *You sure you're Swedish and not Jewish? Have a seat, Miss Durante! Holly wanna cracker?* But judging from the girly magazines Lash shelved toward the back of the shop... Holly braced herself. "What?"

He bounced his eyebrows like Groucho Marx. "Why no 'S' on your chest?"

Holly could have kissed him, he was giving her a punchline! She Grouchoed her eyebrows right back at him. "Because my up-arrow chest logo says that my eyes are up HERE!"

Lash threw back his head and barked a laugh: "HAH! I'm pulling your leg, I know your supersuit's the one in your graphic novel. It made me cry a little. The novel, I mean."

"Thanks." She felt better. She looked at the clock. She felt worse.

The front door dinged. Ann the hairdresser—still so slim and makeup so perfect—carted in two five gallon jugs from Hardware Hank's. "Oof! I could use some help here!"

Holly stood up. "Ann!" It had been a year.

Ann gasped. "Holly! Your hair!" She ran to Holly and embraced her. "You poor, poor thing!"

"Thanks. I can use a hug right now." Holly snuggled into Ann's comforting arms, it felt so much like how Holly's mom used to hold her, so long ago. Holly sniffed, broke the hug, grabbed the jugs, and poured into the metal sink. "But I have a deadline. What is this stuff?"

Ann and Lash donned filter masks.

Lash stuck a broom handle into the sink and stirred. "Oilman Ollie told me how he cleaned drills fast. Hydrocarbon dissolver and a hint of acid." His eyes lit up like a wicked warlock's. "Double, double, toil and, um, crumple? Damn, forgot my Shakespeare."

No mere solvent could harm Holly, but the fumes tickled her nose. "Is there anyone in town you don't know?"

"The bald-headed bowling league." Lash blinked at the smoking stub he'd pulled out of the bubbling brew. "I needed a new broom anyhow."

He and Ann put on arm-length rubber gloves. Two mad doctors about to install a brain into a soon-to-be reanimated corpse.

Lash pointed to the sink. "Holly, go soak your head."

Ann gaped at Lash. "Wait. How long can she hold her breath?"

"With a deep enough breath," Holly said with a little superpowered pride, "I could rescue orbiting astronauts." She inhaled, then plunged her head into solvent. She must look like a ostrich, except she had better looking legs.

Twenty fingers kneaded her scalp. The ***BLURBLE-SLURGLE-FFFSSSHHH*** of sizzling solvent muffled Lash and Ann's conversation, but not Holly's writer imagination. *"Hee hee, Henchwoman Ann, see how we melt the superheroine's brain with my evil bubbling brew! Soon, she will be my obedient, brain-bleached bimbo!" "Yes, Master Lash, yesssss! Hahahahaha!"*

After minutes that passed like hours, Lash tapped Holly's shoulder. She carefully stood up, trying not to splash or drip. Lash asked, "You okay?"

Her sinuses seltzered like she'd snorted boiling dandruff shampoo. Childhood memories of summertime pollen itched her nostrils. "Yeah, but... ***SNIFF!***... feels like my hay fever's coming back... ***AH, AHHH, AH-CHOO!***"

Oh no! Holly reached out fast! Giant, translucent blue hands and arms extended from her flesh-and-blood hands and arms and caught Lash and Ann before they bashed into the ceiling. She gently lowered them to the floor. "Sorry. My sneezes are superpowered now."

Ann frowned. "Cover your mouth next time."

Lash chuckled. "So that's what your super-telekinesis looks like! Let's rinse."

Holly leaned over the sink. "My teke comes in handy. Lets me bench-press army tanks without ripping off two fistfuls of armor."

Lash washed solvent off her head. "Yeah, yeah, you've said comic books were screwing physics for years." He imitated Holly's righteous fangirl voice: "'Human-size hands can't lift a whale-size battleship,'" and Ann joined in, "'even if you're Superman!'"

Holly straightened up and pouted at the two un-fans. "Well, he can't!"

Lash turned off the water. He waved a tissue at Holly. "Need to blow?"

"No." Holly sniffed. "Maybe. This day sucks. I even had to do sports."

Ann turned to Lash and smiled. "She's storytelling again, isn't she?"

"Just like old times," Lash said. Behind him, dozens of football banners and baseball caps lined the apex of wall mirror and ceiling. Holly frowned. *Tribalism. Ugh.*

THE STREET BEFORE THE BANK. 3:49 P.M.

Super Holly was a double-mitted baseball catcher fielding high and outside pitches, her giant telekinetic hands scooping up flying, flailing cops before they splashed into the ocean or splatted on buildings. She set them down behind the surrounding police line and whirled to face the jerk at ground zero. "You lumbering lummox! You could've killed them!"

Harry puffed out his chest like he owned the road. Seven feet tall, five feet wide, a muscle-bound brick wall with a matching I.Q. Tree trunk arms and legs. Battleship armor pectorals. Cauldron of a belly. Moon of a head fronted by a stupidly pleased face. Close-cropped hair so no one could grab it during fights, he picked a lot of those. Torn white shirt falling off. Ripped black pants thankfully staying on. No shoes or socks on those fee-fie-foe-fum feet.

He laughed like a burping foghorn. "BUH-WAH HAW HAW! HARRY HURL PUNY COPS!"

BANG! A young cop shot Harry in the mouth.

PAH-TOOEY! Harry spat the bullet back.

DOINK! It hit the cop on the forehead and knocked him out cold. **PLOP!**

An older cop shook his head. "Damn rookie."

Harry looked down his nose at Holly. "HARRY GONNA ROB BANK! GONNA GRAB MONEY, GET A GIRLFRIEND, BUY TEN POUND STEAK, AND NOT LEAVE TIP! NOW HARRY LEAVE BIG FAT FOOTPRINTS ON YELLOW HAIR'S BIG FAT—"

"Talk to the hands!" yelled Holly. She punched twice. Two bowling-ball-size blue fists cannonballed at Harry's big fat mouth.

And missed because Harry had bent way, way back like a hippo doing the limbo. When had he learned to do THAT?

KERR-RUNCH! SKKKKKTT! A parked car behind Harry had skidded onto the sidewalk, its driver-side door caved in. Holly grit her teeth. Good thing her super-job had liability insurance.

"BAH-WAH HAW HAW! YELLOW HAIR MISS!" Harry stuck out his tongue at Holly: "NNNNN!"

Holly boxer-posed, she was fine with up close and personal. "Fine! You want to rob the bank, you gotta go through me!"

Harry stomped toward Holly like an elephant. Then he winced, like a tiny thought had burst in his B.B. of a brain. He stopped next to a heap of fresh asphalt. He crossed his arms and defiantly glared at Holly. "NO."

Holly kept her guard up. "What do you mean, no?"

Harry lifted his chin. "HARRY NOT LISTEN TO YELLOW HAIR. YELLOW HAIR JUST A GIRL." He snorted, a derisive truck backfiring. "LITTLE GIRLY

GIRL. PUNY. TINY. EXCEPT..." His eyes found Holly's chest. And widened. "WHERE SHE BIG AND ROUND."

Holly's intestines curdled. She closed her mouth in time to stop her jaw from dropping past her knees. *Oh, no. Please, no. Not him. Anybody but him.*

Harry's head bobbled as he rollercoastered his leer over Holly's every curve. "YUM, YUM! HARRY LIKE WHAT HE SEE! LONG LEGS! SMALL WAIST! BIG CHEST! WANNA DATE?"

Holly shuddered, it felt like Harry's eyes had left a slimy slug trail all over her. "Ew! No!"

"YELLOW HAIR LIKE BIG MUSCLE?" Harry bodybuilder-posed and flexed his biceps with a base drum sound: **BOM, BOM!** "CUMMERE AND GIVE HARRY A LITTLE SMACK! KISSY, KISSY!" He smacked his lips, sounding like a toilet plunger working on a clog.

A few cops stifled laughter. Paparazzi zoomed their lenses.

Holly gagged. "Stop that!" She upped her boxer stance to heavyweight. "Or I'll give you a smack, all right!"

"WHY DON'T YELLOW HAIR MAKE HARRY STOP? IS YELLOW HAIR, UHHH, YELLOW? BAH-WAH HAW HAW!" Harry blew a motorcycle-revving super-raspberry: "BBBBBTTTHHHHHPPPPP, BBBPPPP, BBBPPPP, BBBTHHHPPPPPP!"

Bullseye. Holly's face tried to crawl out from under a pint of super spittle. Gasping, trembling, she wiped—*gross, gross, GROSS!*—and flicked gooey saliva off her hand—*ew, ew, EW!* Her steely muscles trembled. Her telekinesis quaked road and

11

atmosphere to make Darth Vader jealous. Inside her mind, she composed, *Get on your knees, hands behind your head, and... OH, THE HECK WITH IT!* Out of her mouth, she roared, "Mff, glerk, snrt, RRRRRAAWLLL!"

She flew at Harry, rocketing her fist at his fat face as...

LASH'S PLACE. 4:48 P.M.

"...steam rocketed out her nose!" Holly sighed. "That happens now when I get really mad."

Lash toweled her head. "Maybe you should've asked yourself why Harry was hitting on you instead of hitting you."

Holly got up and faced the wall mirror. "Hindsight is easy... oh no. NO!"

She wasn't a medusa any more, she was Phyllis Diller after changing hairstyles by sticking a wet finger in a wall socket. The asphalt was gone, but Holly's hair was a knotted, tornado-twisted haystack topped by a hairy golf ball. Dry gasps scraped her throat, her pulse pounded her eardrums. *Calm down!* The clock slammed onto her retinas: 4:49:11, 4:49:12, 4:49:13. *CALM DOWN!*

Holly pulled her steel wire brush out of her yellow hip purse. "I gotta comb! NOW!" She super-strength ***YANK, YANK, YANKED!***

Ann scowled at her. "Holly, you need detangler first."

"No I don't!" An icky memory itched. ***YANK, YANK YANK YANK!*** Holly backed away, bounced off a barber chair, whew, she hadn't broken it. "I can do this!"

She was doing it! Knot after knot came out. Just the

smaller knots, but if she used a tougher tool... Holly grabbed a huge pair of scissors from a shelf and stuck it into that large, nasty knot on top of her head. She pulled and pulled and grr, GRR, GRRRRRED!!!

Lash barked, "Hey, those're my favorite... okay, they're old, but they're still my scissors! And you're gonna tear your hair!"

"My hair's stronger than steel!" Holly bumped into a barber chair. It spun like a top.

Lash pushed his face into Holly's. "Then how come it hasn't grown past your knees?"

"My hair only grows when it has to, just like Superman's!" Holly drilled the scissor blades into the knotted hairy fist crowning her cranium. She would DEFEAT IT!

Lash kept up super-battle banter surprisingly well. "So you shaved your legs just before you went super?"

"As a matter of fact, I did!" Holly yanked hard. The knot didn't budge.

Ann rushed at Holly with fire in her eyes and a bottle in her hand, bobbing and weaving like a boxer looking for an opening. "You hold still, or so help me, I'll spank you!"

Holly pried at the knot as her lips skinned back. Ooo, those bullies who'd ambushed her in fourth grade and held her down and broke her nose and rubbed cow patty into her hair, but she'd fought her way up again and busted all their noses too! Then Uncle Pops had taken her to Lash, who washed away stinky poop and angry tears. Then Ann had poured that goopy detangler on her hair, its stink had slimed into Holly's nostrils like two rotten slugs, Holly had punched Ann's nose, Ann had spanked Holly's butt, and Holly had thrown up for the first time ever. "Ann, you'll just hurt yourself! I'm twenty five and six-foot-one and SUPER now!" She *YANK, YANK, YANKED,* harder, harder, HARDER!

Ann and Holly ping-ponged about the shop. Lash was a spry referee, blocking them from mirrors, shelved decorative beer bottles and sports trophies, and some stacked up Playgal magazines. He was smiling. It figured that he'd like girl fights.

SWAT! Ann had spanked Holly! *BLP-PTT-PTT-PTT, PFFFFFT!* And gooped her!

Grease slithered down Holly's scalp. Her sinuses shivered. She reigned in her retching reflex: if she vomited with her super-strength, she'd blow a hole in the wall.

Ann grasped her hand in pain and looked daggers at Holly.

Holly stiffened her lips. "Sorry! But I've told you what happened," *YANK YANK YANK*, "when Pa Kent tried to spank Superbaby! *YANK-YANK-YANK-YANK-YANK-YANK-YANK-YANK! TWKK-FFT-TWAAANNNG!*

Oops. Really big oops. Lash's left sideburn was half an inch higher than his right, the victim of a broken-off scissor blade embedded in the wall. He glared at Holly so hard she was grateful he didn't have heat vision.

A tidal wave of shame engulfed Holly. "I'm sorry I'm sorry I'm sorry! I never wanted superpowers, I hate my super-job, I hate my supersuit climbing up my butt, why can't I just be a writer again?" She stomped her foot: *THOOOOOMMMM!*

Lash steadied shampoo bottles about to rattle off the shelves. "You're worse than Herman Munster."

Ann stroked Holly's cheek. "Poor thing. Why don't you get a new supersuit?"

"This is the only suit on Earth tough enough for my job." Holly's heartbeat slowed, easing the base-drumming in her ears. When she'd stopped a giant heat ray from frying a bunch of fanboys, she'd worn a cotton T-shirt and jeans. The aftermath had been embarrassing.

"Holly, look over here," Lash said, pointing to the wall. Amid photos of actors, actresses, cops, cheerleaders, radio hosts, football players, sports announcers, and Lash's kids and grandkids, was a photo of a gawky, pre-teen girl. Short brown hair, convex arching nose, excited smile, big blue eyes, and a Batman T-shirt. She had her arm around Lash's waist. He had his arm around her shoulders. With her other arm, she thrust forward a book titled, "Stories of Super Gals!" The photo was signed, "My first sale! Holly Hansson!" And in different handwriting, "My favorite geek girl. Lash."

Oh. Wow. Getting superpowers, her graphic novel going bestseller, saving the world, they had all been thrilling. But Holly would never forget the joy of selling her first short story, *Batty Girl Boxes a Bully*.

Lash's hand settled on Holly's shoulder. "Holly, you're not a little tomboy anymore. You're a grown-up writer AND super woman, and you need my grown-up hairstylist. Now face the music, young lady."

Ann's schoolteacher stare felt like a shrinking ray.

Holly slunk toward the hairdressing chair. "Ann. I'm so sorry. This bad hair day really messed me up."

Ann did a surprisingly good Yoda. "It's more than that. Your temper, your temper, you must control your temper!"

Holly nodded. "I should have done that earlier today. But instead, Harry and I slugged and snorted like..."

THE STREET BEFORE THE BANK. 3:53 P.M.

...two heavyweight boxers with a two-decade grudge! Harry pachyderm-pounded Holly's face, knocking her a few feet back with each blow. But for each blow, Holly yo-yoed forward and clobbered him with five! ***THOOM! POW POW POW POW POW! THOOM!! POW POW POW POW POW!! THOOM!!! POW POW POW POW POW!!!***

Harry laughed like a schoolyard bully. "BAH-WAH HAW— FMMMFF!" A bully with a fist in his kisser. "YELLOW HAIR HIT LIKE GIRL! KISSY KISSY— OOF OOF OOF!"

Holly's right-left-right jabs to a big pot belly stoked the fire in her gut. She hopped back and bent her legs.

A cop blared through a bullhorn. Bennie the Rubber Cop, Holly knew that world-weary voice. "KID, THE SUPER-STUN CANNON IS HERE! BACK OFF AND GIVE US A SHOT!"

"He's MINE!" Holly uncoiled her left leg, adding every iota of ultra-super-duper power to her right-leg kick. Her telekinetic foot—ten times actual size— slammed into Harry's crotch. Feedback ran up Holly's leg and roiled her rump: ***BLOOOOOOMMMMMBBBB!***

Holly shook the ringing out of her ears. That hadn't sounded right.

Harry's eyes crossed. "HARRY... FALL..." He timbered back and dented the pavement: **KER-KRUMMMP!**

Holly flexed her toes. Hadn't felt right either. She leaned over the mound of muscle. Whose arms were spread. Eyes shut. Split lip. Sweaty muscle chest... which wasn't moving!

She leaned closer. She'd clobbered Harry before. But never on THAT bullseye. She looked to the cops. "Is there a doctor in the house?"

Bennie bullhorned, "LOOK OUT!"

A meaty arm clamped onto her neck. Holly twisted, but was held praying-mantis tight. Ew, a mantis that needed deodorant.

A big mouth thundered in her ear. "BAH-WAH HAW HAW! YOU DUMB! HARRY HELD BREATH! YOUR KICK NOT HURT HARRY! HARRY WEARING SUPER-ARMORED JOCKSTRAP! SEE?" *CLANG, CLANG!*

Holly did not try to see. *That better have been his finger!* She pawed at the vise on her neck, but could not grip its sweaty skin. Wait, not sweaty, OILY! *Who oils up for a fight*— and she knew. She asked anyhow. "Where'd you learn these moves?"

"WRESTLERS!" Harry crowed the word. "THEY LOUD. RUDE. MEAN. FUN!"

Of course. A slab of beef hiding amid slabs of beef. Holly couldn't aim a punch or kick. But she could flex! She tensed her arms and shoulders, sending out a telekinetic blast that could shatter a steel girder.

Harry's arm stayed firm as an elephant's leg. "BAH-

WAH HAW HAW! YELLOW HAIR'S STRENGTH SLIP OFF OILY SKIN!"

"Then how come I can't slip out?"

"GLUE INSIDE ELBOW!"

Oh, brother. Holly bent her legs for a bound-over-a-building leap, to be followed by her copyrighted bash-herself-and-big-bully-into-the-street landing. "Up, up, and—"

She tried to jump. She stayed earthbound. But why? She looked down.

Harry's toes were dug into the road like oak tree roots. That loudmouth was just full of ideas today! "BAH-WAH HAW HAW! YELLOW HAIR CAN'T MOVE HARRY! HARRY LIKE ROCK OF GIBRUH, GIBBER, GIB-UH-WALTER, UH..."

Holly hollered, "Rock of Gibraltar, you moron!"

Harry hollered, "STOP THAT! BIG WORDS HURT HARRY'S HEAD!"

Holly slammed her head back. **KRRRMP!** Yes! Feedback from butthead nose to the back of her cranium felt REALLY GOOD!

"FNUFF!" snorted Harry. His oily torso slickly twisted on Holly's cheek as his free arm reached toward the nearby asphalt heap. Then his boxing-glove hand smacked her skull, reminding her of when she was learning to boogie-board and a wave had slammed her headfirst into the beach and it had taken three days until she could look over her shoulder again. Ow ow OW.

Tar vapor smoked into her lungs. TAR?!?!? *NOT MY HAIR!* She raked super-fingernails on Harry's arm. "rrrrRRRR!"

"YOU CHEAT! NO SCRATCH!" Harry's bicep ballooned, compressing Holly's windpipe so air molecules trickled down single file. "NOW HARRY USE BIGGEST BADDEST WRESTLING MOVE OF ALL TIME!"

Holly's mind raced. Sleeper hold? Elbow cracker? Eye gouger? Belly bopper?

A fist bashed atop her head and twisted. The knuckles were pounding pile drivers. Harry howled, "NOOGIE NOOGIE NOGGIE NOOGIE NOOGIE!"

Holly squirmed and screeched like a cat in a blender. She tried and failed to bite Harry's arm. Oh well, it would have taken gallons of mouthwash to gargle away the taste of butthead.

A low growl: "HARRY KNOW YELLOW HAIR LOVE HER YELLOW HAIR." A loud roar: "NOW HARRY DESTROY YELLOW HAIR'S YELLOW HAIR! NOOGIE NOOGIE NOOGIE NOOGIE NOOGIE! HARRY LIKE REVENGE! NOOGIE NOOGIE NOOGIE!"

LASH'S PLACE. 4:54 P.M.

"It felt like Shrub Oil was drilling into my brain, with the usual lack of safety regulations." Holly settled back into the hairdressing chair, head over the sink. The detangler had done its job. Ann had guided her brushing: "Grab the base of that knot. Dig the comb in above your fingers. Now use your super-strength, gently but firmly, and pull. Easy, steady, and careful." Holly had broken three stainless steel combs, two on that last big knot on top of her head.

But those nasty knots were gone, all gone. And a beautiful bouquet blossomed in Holly's nose. "Oh,

Ann. You remembered."

"You do love strawberries." Ann worked in pink suds and sang, "Gonna wash that jerk right out of your hair, gonna wash that jerk right out of your hair."

Mmm, those magic fingers, that sweet scent, that angelic tune... Holly closed her eyes. Her tension melted.

"Gonna wash... um..." Ann trailed off.

Holly sighed dreamily. "Could you massage my neck?"

"Holly?"

The hairdressing chair softened into a cloud. "My muscles... **SIGH**... are like steel..." *Strawberry pillows forever.* "But if you knead real hard..."

"HOLLY!"

Holly's eyes snapped open. She was floating a couple of feet above the chair. She fell back down with a ***PLOP!***

"HA!" Lash counted the cash register's daily take. "Whirlybird Willy told me you nearly got a ticket for sleep-floating."

"Ever since his police helicopter woke me up with 'ATTENTION, UNIDENTIFIED SNORING OBJECT,' I tuck myself in at night." Holly checked her e-bracelet. 4:56. *Yes! We're gonna make it!*

Warm water soothed her scalp. Ann's tune soothed her soul. "Gonna rinse the soap right out of your hair, while you end your story with your usual flair."

Holly winked at Ann. "You're picking up on story structure. So, Holly thrashed and kicked..."

THE STREET BEFORE THE BANK. 4:05 P.M.

...and screamed, "Stop it stop it stop it stop it STOP IT!"

Harry's knuckles bobbled Holly's brain. "NOOGIE NOOGIE NOOGIE NOOGIE NOOGIE!" He stopped grinding his knuckles, shoved his face close, and yelled, "HARRY DIDN'T REALLY WANNA DATE YOU!" Yuck, he needed a five-pound breath mint.

Holly yelled, "So you didn't mean all that stuff about how I look?"

Harry yelled, "NO! WHEN HARRY LOOK AT YELLOW HAIR, HE ONLY SEE STRONG, BRAVE, HATED ENEMY!"

Holly yelled, "Thank you!"

Harry yelled, "YOU WELCOME!" Argh, Harry's knuckles dug in again! "NOOGIE NOOGIE NOOGIE NOOGIE NOOGIE!"

The police line split open, revealing a howitzer of a ray-gun, its massive muzzle glowing and ready. Holly had never been so happy to be looking down a gun barrel. She waited, and waited, and waited, and where was the big boom? She shouted as her teeth rattled, "W-w-w-what are you waiting for? Sh-sh-sha-shoot!"

Bennie bullhorned, "KID! YOU'LL BE KNOCKED OUT TOO!"

Asphalt grit ground into her pores. "I can take that, but I can't take this butthead for another nanosecond! DO IT!"

Bennie sounded excruciatingly sad. "YOU HEARD THE LADY. HIT IT."

THA-THOOOMMMM!!! A flash of light, a clap of thunder, a bulldozer slamming the air out of her lungs. ***THA-THOOOMMMM!!! THA-THOOOMMMM!!!***

THA-THOOOoooo...

Blackness...

LASH'S PLACE. 4:58 P.M.

"I was unconscious for a few minutes." Holly sat up straight, making her head a better target for Ann's humming blowdryer. "The cops hauled off Harry. I felt my hair and I screamed. Bennie comforted me with a hug, hankies for my tears, and a wisecrack. 'Anything I can do, kid? Iced mocha? Batman comic books? Bullets in some paparazzi?' I told him, 'Thanks, but only one man can save me now.' Then I flew here, and the rest is history."

Ann finished the last brush strokes. She turned the chair, facing Holly at the wall mirror. "Look at the lovely superwoman."

Oh! Holly ran her fingers through her long, lustrous, sunshiny, silky soft, full-and-bouncy blond hair. She stuffed a fistful to her nose—***SNNNMMFFFFFFF!***—and was grateful that her deviated septum still let her inhale lots of sweet strawberry scent. "HAHHHHHHHHH!"

Holly leaped out of the chair and hugged Ann. "Thank you!"

Then she kissed Lash on the cheek—"MMM-WAH!"—while lifting him off his feet with a super-hug. "And thank you, you old goat!"

"You're welcome," Lash wheezed, "please put me down."

Holly did. "Sorry." She pulled a couple bills out of her hip purse and handed them to Lash. "Will this cover it?"

Lash took them. "Yeah."

Holly checked her e-bracelet.

Three seconds to five o'clock.

Two.

One.

DING-A-LING went the front doorbell.

An inky-black specter filled the front doorway like John Wayne's ghost.

Goose pimples scampered on Holly's thighs and forearms. She set herself between the door and the innocent bystanders.

Light dimmed. Air thickened. The shadow slid forward, silent as smoke. Its Dracula eyes seared Holly's soul, its Shakespearian voice shivered her spine. "Holly Hansson. I have come for you."

Through the open door, from a clear blue sky, a bolt of lightning ***KRACK-KOOMED!***

The shadow spread its cape into devil wings emerging from hell's deepest pit.

Holly reached out to the cowled man in the black body-armor costume, complete right down to bullet-proof six-pack abs. He embraced Holly with a flutter of his cape. They kissed with a flutter of Holly's heart. *Oh, his arms! Yum, his lips! Ooo, that kevlar!*

Lash made the moment perfect. "Careful, Holly, your nose might poke his eye out!"

The man broke the kiss. He still loomed over Holly even though he was two inches shorter. "I am your teacher. I am your critic. I am... YOUR DATE!"

Holly batted her eyes. "Yes, Cal."

Lash and Ann harmonized. "Holly's gotta boyfriend!"

"And an occasional janitor," Cal said. He withdrew a pill from his utility belt and tossed it into the solvent-filled sink. "My Intellecta-anti-pollution pill." He took off his cowl and approached Lash with outstretched hand. "California Critbert. Now also known as 'The Intellectual.' Pleasure to meet you."

Lash shook Cal's hand and beamed. "I've been a huge fan of your movie reviews for years! You asked the same question I did about that last Superman movie."

Cal nodded. "How did Clark Kent shave off invulnerable beard stubble? I thought barbers would spot that."

Holly said, "Cal? Our date?"

Lash whiffed the solvent. "Smells like roses. How'd you know my sink would be gunked up?"

Cal raised his teaching finger. "Elementary olfactory deduction, my dear barber. My enhanced sense of smell detected acid, tar, and—"

ONE MINUTE LATER!
Lash looked at Holly but did not say goodbye. "Mr. Critbert, how'd you know Holly'd be here? Your enhanced hearing catch her temper tantrum?"

Holly pouted. "I said I was sorry."

Cal lectured his new student. "I almost homed in on Holly's e-bracelet, but then I calculated—"

ANOTHER MINUTE LATER!
Holly crossed her arms. "Cal, the Geek Guy's will close in—"

Lash looked out the front door, his forehead

wrinkling. "How'd you cue that lightening without a magic hammer?"

Cal opened his super-smarty-pants mouth again. *Oh, joy.*

YET ANOTHER MINUTE LATER!
Thunder and lightening outside again. After wind, rain, and a pink elephant parade. Lash blinked. "Wow. You just think, and you get special effects?"

Cal tapped his cranium. "Yes. Telepathic link to the Intellecta-car's holographic projector."

Ann sighed. "Boys and their toys."

Holly's gaze was a lousy tractor beam, Cal was NOT coming! "I want him to toy with something else!"

Lash looked up to a couple of large speakers mounted above his big wooden desk. "Say, smart guy..."

Holly clenched her jaw. *Oh, no.*

Lash looked sourly down at his desktop Apricot computer, a conundrum he had never quite mastered. "I never got my speakers to work with this thing."

Cal cracked his knuckles, and with a flourish of black cape, he sat down at Lash's desk. "A tweak of the wireless setting should do it. What's your system password?"

Lash shuffled though a stack of papers on his desk. "Uh, I wrote it down somewhere."

Cal typed with blinding speed. "No matter. I'll program and run a decrypting algorithm."

Holly looked at Ann. Ann looked at Holly. Their thoughts matched without the aid of telepathy: *Men!*

Holly puffed out her chest, squared her shoulders,

and jutted her jaw.

Ann stifled a laugh. "You're stretching your chest logo."

"HOLLY NOT CARE!" bellowed Holly. She elephant-stomped to her knight in kevlared armor, scooped him out of the desk chair, cradled him like a baby, and laughed in his face. "BAH-WAH HAW HAW! HOLLY GRAB DATE!"

Cal raised an eyebrow. "Your vocabulary has suddenly devolved."

Holly hollered in her beloved's face. "HOLLY WANT DATE! WANT PICK UP WEEKLY COMIC BOOKS, EAT PACHO VILLA BEAN SOUP, TAKE LONG WALK ON BEACH, WATCH OCEAN SUNSET, AND DO LOTSA KISSY KISSY!"

Cal's big brown eyes smoldered. "You have defeated me. By learning from Harry Headbutt. I love you."

Lash threw his head back and guffawed. "HAH! How do you like your new job now, Holly?"

Holly stopped as she carried her prize through the front door. She kissed Cal hard: "Mmmmm!" Then she winked over her shoulder at Lash. "HOLLY LIKE JOB BENEFITS!"

2 THE POET AND THE SUPERSPLAINER!

SEASIDE CITY, CALIFORNIA. ONE HUNDRED FEET UP AND HALF A MILE NORTH OF THE APRICOT COMPUTER CAMPUS. A FRIDAY. 3:17 P.M.

Supersplain. [soop-er-spleyn] Verb. Instruct a superhero (usually a female one) on how to perform every single detail of her job as though she'd never punched a supervillain, or never saved a civilian, or never even read a superhero comic book in her entire life! Usually performed by a male superhero of the Batman variety, and Super Holly Hansson gritted her teeth at Cal "The Intellectual" Critbert's constant supersplaining as Holly flew toward the Apricot Campus.

"Tilt twenty two degrees toward the breeze, your cape will billow more impressively that way! Remember not to tug on your costume's rear or henchmen will wolf-whistle! And stay behind me when you land, the one who inspires the most fear must lead the charge!" Cal's grim, on-the-job voice sent a shiver up Holly's spine despite the bright warm day, thanks to the audio-perfect Intellecta-earphone Cal had lent her.

"How about inspiring me with why we're crashing the A-phone press conference?" Ten minutes ago, Cal's cowled 3-D holographic visage had leaped out of Holly's e-bracelet like a Jack-in-the-Box. She'd spilled her iced mocha on the third draft of her next comic book script. Now she spotted and flew toward the Apricot Computer Theater. Only Chris Jobz could have designed a giant apricot-shaped dome to look good amid high-tech office buildings.

Cal said why. "5-D."

Oh, no! Comic Convent memories doubled Holly's blood pressure. Corrupted fanboys! Evil fangirls! Brain-eating movies! And a movie critic who became the love of her life and the yin to her yang and her teacher and critic and a great kisser. 5-D? Jobz wouldn't DARE!

Holly flew in for a landing. Ooo, yes, the long black scary sleekness of the Intellecta-car was in the parking lot. Along with police cars. And a few unconscious cops. This was a job for Super Holly. "I'll go in first. I'm bulletproof."

"So is my Intellecta-body armor."

"I've got super-strength!"

"I have super-speed!"

"Only in short bursts!" Holly landed at the theater entrance. "What are you doing?"

Cal was hunched at the apricot-shaped door, his hands hidden by his black cape and cowl. He murmured dark-alley low, "Picking the lock."

This was no time to dawdle. Holly smacked her

palm on the thick steel door.

BAH-WHAMMM! The door flew off its hinges.

Cal's big brown eyes bored into Holly's soul. "I calculate a sixty-seven percent probability that our insurance rates will go up. Now analyze the battlefield with me." He dashed inside, his black cape billowing like a thundercloud about to engulf evildoers. One of those billows revealed how nicely Cal's body armor accentuated his buns. Yummy.

Holly used a touch of her telekinesis to put extra flutter into her red cape. Even with her lifetime of reading comic books and writing superhero stories, she was still adjusting to her new super-job. Cal, however, had slipped into the dark knight role with ease. Were movie critics more adaptable than comic book writers? Was mid-thirties more mature than mid-twenties? No, he wasn't! She levitated to peek over Cal, opening her eyes wider to adjust to dimmer light. "There's—"

"Victims: check!" Cal's super-fast mind and even faster mouth beat Holly to it. He pointed to the unconscious reporters, security guards, and cops strewn throughout the auditorium.

Holly growled, "I see that!"

"Minions: check!" Cal pointed to the couple of dozen ninjas charging at them.

"I see them too!"

"Famously arrogant CEO, prototype 5-D A-phone, and lead supervillainess: check!" Tall, slim, and black-turtlenecked Chris Jobz knelt by the center stage podium before a white karate-gi-robed woman. His prayer-folded hands offered the phone to the lady. His eyes overflowed with dreamy worship.

"I see it!" But Holly didn't believe it!

Cal raised his right arm, aiming his grappling hook for a dramatic swoop to the stage. Just like last week, when he'd finally given in to Holly's pleading and kissing and batting of her big blue eyes. For nearly an hour, they had swung from tall building rooftop to rooftop, Cal's right arm shooting his Intellecta-grappling hook, his left holding Holly close. Holly had hugged her black-caped Tarzan close on every swoop through the darkening night. Best lovers embrace EVER!

Then Cal spoiled the memory. "You take the minions, I'll take the greater danger."

"Oh no, you don't!" Holly flew over Cal, timing it just right... *Yes!* His grappling hook bounced off Holly's stronger-than-steel tummy, he wasn't swooping anywhere today! Holly landed on the stage and yelled, "She's MINE!" Whoever the heck she was.

Cal's voice vibrated Holly's earphone with resonance that terrified the toughest of crooks. "The Karate Queen. Age: 32. Weight: 139 pounds. Height: 5 foot 8. Hair: brunette. Powers: super martial arts. Superpower Category: 1-A!"

1-A? Capable of harming me? Well, I can harm army tanks! Holly turned away from Cal and the wave of ninjas about to swallow him, and boy, were they gonna get it! Holly landed a cautious ten feet from the Karate Queen. She tugged at her blue supersuit's rear to prevent any wedgies in the upcoming battle and faced the villainess.

A ninja wolf-whistled.

The Karate Queen scratched Chris behind the ear, making him wriggle like a happy puppy. Her smile was pretty confident for someone facing the mightiest super on Earth. She chanted, "One of you against one of me? You abandon your partner with careless glee."

A rhyming villainess. Might be a nice change from the banter Holly was getting lately. *HARRY SMUSH! My ice cream shall f-f-f-freeze every brain in town, heh heh heh! Ew, you're a big meanie but the boys like me, me, ME! STOP SAYING STUFF, BIG WORDS HURT HARRY'S HEAD!* Holly adjusted her boxer pose to welterweight, then cocked her head toward the buffalo-like rumbling in the auditorium seats. "Does he look like he needs help?"

The Karate Queen did not put up her dukes. She turned. Her smile expanded.

Holly had to take just one quick little peek too! *Mmm, yes!* Cal was a dark whirlwind tearing through the evil horde. **BIFF! BOP! POW! BAM!**

An increasingly unhappy evil horde. Ninjas plummeted and plopped, flew and flopped, and otherwise fell victim to Cal's flashing fists and feet. A beautiful, brutal ballet. "Ouch!" "Oof!" "Ugh!" "I thought this guy only had normal strength!" *Go, my Batman, go!*

Holly's headset howled, "EYES on your OPPONENT!"

"All right, all right!" *Spoilsport!* Holly tightened her fists and gave the Karate Queen her complete attention and when this was over she was going to make Cal put a volume control on this stupid earphone! "Stop petting the CEO and surrender."

The martial arts mistress glanced at Chris. "Continue to program the app, my boy, here's a blond bimbo that I shall destroy."

Chris kissed her feet: ***MMM-WAH, MMM-WAH!*** "Yes, my goddess, yes!" He danced his fingers on the phone with Silicon Valley intensity.

"This BLONDE," Holly spat the word, so much for poetry, "can punch through battleship armor. If you don't have super-strength, you better have super health insurance." She did a fear-inspiring glare, Cal having fine-tuned that during last week's sparring lesson. *Holly, hold nothing back, not your fists, not your gaze. You've learned to pull your punches with normal-strength people so you won't pulp them. I know that, you know that, but villains need not know that!*

The proud poet raised her arms in a karate pose, bent her legs slightly, did a come-get-some gesture with her right hand, and it was about time! "My spiritual chi powers me. Does your super-strength hold up your triple-D's?"

That match lit burners in Holly's cheeks. She got bust-line cracks from paparazzi, now this kung-fu quack too? She cocked her arm for a super right hook. "Talk—"

Before she could finish her "Talk to the hands" catchphrase, Cal's command ice-picked her diamond-tough eardrum. "Never announce your upcoming move! And fight her from a distance!"

"I wasn't announcing!"

"Yes you were."

Later, Holly would ask Cal why movie critics hated catchphrases. She reached out as if to straight-arm clap. From her arms and hands extended giant blue transparent arms and hands. Maybe super-telekinesis would grab her majesty!

The Karate Queen gave the most cursory of glances at the two seven-foot-wide, transparent telekinetic hands surrounding her. Then...

She leaped! Snap-kicked! Spun! Roundhouse kicked! Cat-quiet-perfectly landed! And triumphantly smirked!

The two giant hands rippled and vanished.

"Ow, ow, OWWWITCH!" Holly flapped her hands to chase away what felt like two ten-foot wasps attacking her palms. "Do you have any idea how much telekinetic feedback stings? Do you? Hey! LOOK AT ME!"

But the Karate Queen was ogling Cal like J. Wellington Wimpy admiring a hamburger. "Your boyfriend brawls extremely well. Compared to him, your fighting smells."

Holly reared up to her full six-foot-one. The Queen did not look impressed. For the first time in her life, Holly wished she was wearing high heels. "Tell that to that hulking moron Harry Headbutt, or the dozens of super soldiers I clobbered, or—"

BUMP WHUMP BUMPLE THUMP! A ninja tumbled onto the stage, past Holly, and sprawled before the Karate Queen. He coughed, "Medic," and passed out.

Chris boogied his digits on the phone. "App now in alpha phase, my goddess."

What did that martial mama do to him? Holly cocked for a left jab and a right hook. "Let's see how super-karate fares against stronger-than-steel fists!"

"Holly!" said Cal.

"WHAT?" Holly's blood pressure pounded her eardrums.

"Your hair."

Holly groaned. "Do I have to?"

"I can list twenty seven problems relating to lovely long hair in battle, each with their various sub—"

"Please don't." Holly reached into her yellow hip purse. Her opponent's casual stance and amused grin said that she was in no hurry. "Give me a moment," Holly asked anyhow. "You can use it to edit your rhymes. Even though that stuff went out with Underdog cartoons."

Well, well, her majesty's face flinched! Was she touchy about her poetry? Or maybe jealous of Holly's writing success? The Queen quickly recovered her composure and put her hands on her hips. "Certainly, Holly, take your time, while I compose my superior rhymes."

With a blue scrunchie that matched her supersuit and her eyes, Holly tied her long blond hair into a ponytail. "Cal's been bugging me about my hair getting in the way during close combat. Even though most supervillains know to keep their hands off my hair if they want to stay healthy."

The Karate Queen nodded. "So he tells you how to fight. Does he think he's always right?"

Holly boxer-bounced on the balls of her feet. She orbited her fists, revving them up. "He is super-intelligent. And my teacher."

Cal's voice came so compassionate and caring that Holly came close to agreeing with him. "Holly, she is toying with you. Let's trade places before you are hurt. There are still thirteen ninjas you can clobber."

Two ninjas joined the conversation. "UGH!" "ERK!" **PLOP. THUD.**

Cal said, "Make that eleven."

The Queen posed her hands like she was about to swat a fly. "He's so tough, yet so talky! Methinks he could be a bit less bossy!"

Holly had to smile. "Tell me about it. Yesterday I was making my lunch, and Cal instructed me on how to correctly cut my carrot strips."

"He did?" The Karate Queen's eyes went wide. "You kid!"

It was nice to get womanly sympathy about guy stuff, even from a villainess. "Not kidding. When I asked Cal what the heck difference does it make how I slice them, he gave me a two-minute lecture about exposing the maximum carrot cellular structure, thus," Holly took on a condescending tone, "increasing its impact upon my taste buds by eighty six percent!"

The Karate Queen thoughtfully stroked her chin. "Over-precision can be quite a bother! But how to fix him?" She smiled like an evil sorceress, and not the ugly variety. "A better lover!"

Steam puffed out Holly's nose, so much for female bonding! She raised her fists and cocked her right leg. Like HELL she was gonna pull her punches! "He's MINE!"

Cal spoke fast. "Holly, I beg you, BACK OFF! I shall quicken my combat!"

BIFF BAP BOP BAM WHAM went Cal's fists of justice.

"Not so fast! OW OOTCH ERK!" went ninjas of bruises.

Holly sped up too. She flew at the Karate Queen, fists and feet cocked and ready. Time to end this!

A guarding block to Holly's left forearm deflected her left hook, a knife-hand blow to Holly's right ankle parried her roundhouse right kick, and a limbo body bend dodged her vicious head-butt. All in less than two seconds. This villainess put every rubber-backboned battle babe in the movies to shame! The Queen's glowing hands darted like summertime fireflies... great, another childhood memory just went sour.

Holly usually outfought that giant jerk Harry Headbutt by delivering five punches for every one of his. That was not working here. She jabbed and kicked, snarled and growled, and missed and missed and MISSED! "Let me land just one blow, you... you..." Insults boiled in Holly's throat. She spat out the nastiest of all: "You William McGonagall clone!"

The Karate Queen reared back like a cobra and hissed. Hah, so her majesty knew of the worst poet in history! But she calmed down fast. Her mongoose-fast hands parried while the rest of her did not even seem to be breathing hard. She yawned, "Bored now." She jabbed Holly's right arm, leg, and ear, and then she smiled sweetly. "Sore now?"

Porcupine bombs burst in Holly's right arm and leg, which flopped into limp, wet noodle numbness. Holly backed off... and started tipping to the right. But she'd been liberal for years! She levitated leftward. Scenery straightened up. "What the heck was THAT?"

The Karate Queen bowed deeply. "I struck your nerve clusters with super-chi power. You'll throw no right hooks for about an hour."

Cal again. His voice was too heartbroken to rub it in. "I calculate fifty three minutes, fourteen sec—"

BZZZPP!

Holly's earphone fell out and shattered on the floor. She silently mouthed at the Karate Queen, *Thank you*. She turned toward the auditorium seats. "You win, Cal. Let's switch."

A dark shadow turned its back upon seven whimpering ninjas. They shuddered in unison at the **FLOOOFFF** of the shadow's inky cape.

Holly floated away from the Queen and toward the ninjas. Cal flashed past Holly in a somersault-leap onto the stage. And he slapped something onto Holly's face. *Oh no, no, NO!*

Apricot Goggles activated. Cal's cowled, transparent face zoomed into Holly's vision, a ghostly Batman head. "Testing, testing," it said.

Holly was not in the mood for a pop quiz! Stabilizing against her numb right limbs, she floated toward the ninjas and said, "No advice, Cal, I can clobber these guys with one arm tied behind—" Wait. She was one-armed already.

She glanced at the stage, where a dark-caped man and a white-robed woman were dueling propellers. "Cal? Are you all right?"

"I did not utilize my Intellecta-gun, I calculate a ninety seven percent probability that you'd catch the bullets and... I'm fine, Holly. Finish the ninjas. I'll have her checkmated in thirty one seconds." His floating face in Holly's goggles focused on something before him. "Madam, keep your guard up on your left."

Holly sighed. Always the critic. She turned to the ninjas and shook her left fist. "I can bench-press an army tank with one hand. So—"

A ninja grabbed his head. "Ow! Your telekinesis!" He fell sprawling into an auditorium seat and shut his eyes. "It knocked me out!"

Huh? But Holly hadn't... oh. These henchmen weren't so dumb.

The remaining ninjas pratfalled onto the floor and into auditorium seats like dominoes: **THUD PLOP THUMP WHUMP PLOP PLOP!** A flat-on-his-back ninja looked hopefully up at Holly. "Um, we'll just lie here now?"

Holly lowered her fist. "Sure, boys, take it easy." Then Cal's gasp turned her blood to ice.

In Holly's goggles, Cal fearfully choked, "Can't... move... due to brain-numbing super-karate blow!"

A happy, evil warble! "The opera is over, the fast lady sings! I now clip another man's wings!"

Holly spun toward the stage, hissing at phantom razors slicing her right side.

Cal stood statue-rigid. The Karate Queen stroked Cal's cheek with one finger, licked her lips, and purred into his face, "A better henchman I do crave! Prepare to become my lust-soaked slave!"

Holly's heart detonated white-hot rage into every fiber of her body. She missiled at the Karate Queen, except her right-side fins were rubbery. "KEEP AWAY FROM HIM!"

First eye-blink: The Karate Queen ducked a

cannonballing telekinetic left fist! Second eye-blink: She parried a left-leg kick that could have shattered a safe! Third eye-blink: She side-stepped! So FAST!

A million icicles exploded from Holly's spine and tore into her nervous system. The hardwood stage floor swung up and clubbed her square on the nose.

Holly sniffed through cramped nostrils. She tried to roll over, to flex her limbs, to wriggle even a single tendon. Nothing. All lines from her brain to everything below her neck were tingly-numb busy. But her face, she could move that! She pressed her eyebrows together, skinned back her lips to expose grinding teeth, and channeled the heat of her boiling blood into her eyes. Fat lot of good that did, making an angry face for the floorboards. But sooner or later, that karate skank would see it!

From above came a lofty coo. "Time you faced your utter defeat. Only heartache shall you reap!"

Fingers clawed into Holly's hair and yanked. The floor receded. Wow, her beaky super-nose had made quite a divot in the hardwood. The limp-ninja-filled auditorium seats swung into view and grew closer with every bump and scrape of Holly's unfeeling potato-sack body.

Holly sputtered. That vicious vixen was DRAGGING her! By the HAIR! Like a CAVEMAN! Oh, how Holly wanted to twitch her mighty middle finger!

The front row of auditorium chairs were a few feet away. Scenery spun. Holly plopped into a front-and-center chair.

The happily humming Queen bent over and gently adjusted Holly's dishrag body to sit up straight and face center stage. "Nice and comfy you shall be, so my finale you can see!"

Holly glared at the villainess and growled like a rabid dog on an unbreakable chain. *Behold the face of upcoming vengeance!*

The Queen's kind smile did not waver in the slightest. "If looks could kill, I'd be sixty feet under. Now watch me tear his soul asunder." She slinked to the stage, a seductive lioness about to dine.

If only Holly had heat vision, or freezing breath, or even projectile snot! But no. Just super-strength, super-toughness, super-telekinesis, super-healing that was NOT kicking in, and... flight!

She willed herself to fly. *Fly, c'mon, FLY...* she rose... and plopped back into the chair. *DAMMIT, DAMMIT, DAMMIT!*

The Karate Queen grabbed Cal's head like a cat grabbing a mouse. Her ruby red lips glowed. "My darling, have a taste of what I did to Chris! Watch closely Holly, this you don't want to miss!" She glommed hungrily onto Cal's mouth.

Cal stood so still, his face in Holly's goggles was wide-eyed with shock... and then blazed in anger! "Foul temptreff! Won't luff you, I luff..." He pursed his lips. "HOLLY!"

The Queen was knocked back three feet. The Intellecta-karate-kiss! During last week's sparring session, Holly had gotten up and asked for seconds.

In her entire life, Holly had never thought she'd go cheerleader. But she yelled, "You lose! Don't cry! You'll never turn Cal to the henchman side! Um, right, Cal?"

Cal's gaze at the Karate Queen was a laser beam to bore holes in sinister skulls. "Absolutely."

The Queen's gaze at Cal was an ice storm.

Chris Jobz ran to her side, fell to his knees, and handed her the A-phone. "Your 5-D app is now backed by the networked power of thousands of Apricot servers! A gift for my goddess, my mistress, my love, my omniscient operating system, my ultimate user interface, my—"

The Karate Queen stilled Jobz's soliloquy with a touch of her finger on his lips. Then she pointed the phone at Cal. It bathed Cal's head in a sinister glow. "In my 5-D cinema you shall be! 'Man Mashing Mistresses, Number Twenty Three!'"

Holly winced, remembering Cal's review of that kung-fu franchise. *Flying female karate kicks to male craniums enslave dozens of palace guards, seven samurai, and a king, pushing women's lib forward five years. They also reveal enough bosom and butt to push it back five decades. The subtitles had the volume of an Adam West Batman fight, but none of the wit.*

Cal's head snapped like a punching bag, left and right, forward and back, over and over! "Uh! Ow! Ah! Ugh! Urg! Uhhh..." Cal looked so dizzy and weak.

The Karate Queen slithered toward Cal. "Your mind was super-strong, I see!" She wrapped her arms and one leg around her prey. "But now it is no match for me!" Her lips glowed. She kissed hard.

The brave light in Cal's eyes dimmed, and cold fear grew. "No... no... I luff... Holly... luff... Hol... luff... luh..."

Holly felt so helpless! And so MAD! Steam firehosed out her nose! She blinked hard. Her superpowers! Still there! But her telekinesis worked through pantomime, what could she do with it, pout at— *that's it!* But she had to time it just right! Holly yelled with righteous fury, "Hey, you stuck-up, mousey-brown, Xena-wanna-be! My graphic novel is a national bestseller, but your puny poems wouldn't last five seconds in my writer's critique group!"

The Karate Queen's entire body jerked, breaking the evil kiss. Gasping, shaking, snarling with rage, she let go of Cal, turned toward Holly, and screeched, "YOU TAKE THAT BA-"

Now! Holly stuck out her tongue with every atom of super-strength that she could muster: "BBNNNNNNNN!"

"—CKFFFFTTT!" said the Karate Queen as a translucent, telekinetic, blue, boxing-glove sized tongue torpedoed onto her kisser!

The Karate Queen's head snapped back-forward-back-forward like a punching bag, then bobbled to a stop. She swayed, stumbled, then fell flat on her back: **WHUMP!** Her legs kicked up, twitched, and hit the floor: **PLOP!**

Got her! Oh, but my poor, poor Cal! In Holly's goggles, Cal's face was lined and pained, his beautiful brown eyes showed a mind hanging on by its fingernails. "Won't... love... I... Holly..."

Holly blinked to clear her teary vision. *Fly, c'mon, FLY... ow, ow, OOOOOWWWWWWWWW!* Limply, agonizingly, she rose. Slowly, wobblingly, she drifted towards her beloved. At last, his breath puffed upon her lips.

She kissed him. Or rather, she lurched her body

THE POET AND THE SUPERSPLAINER!

forward and mashed her lips on his.

Cal moaned, "Luff... luff... mmmmmmmm."

After a long, loving minute, Holly floated back and looked deep into Cal's eyes. "Are you okay?"

Like a half-Vulcan science officer, Cal raised his right eyebrow. Like a movie critic after feasting upon Casablanca, his eyes twinkled. "Your soulmate kiss jump-started my brain." He took Holly's limp hand and kissed it. "You saved me. Thank you."

Holly suppressed a pout. Batman was supposed to save Superman, not the other way around. "You're welcome. Now can you save me an hour of super-healing? This pincushion numbness is killing me!"

Cal flexed his fingers, then aimed them at her like kung-fu scalpels. "Certainly. I have calculated the Intellecta-pokes to your nerve clusters that will restore you. Our soulmate connection will prevent your super-toughness from harming my fingertips." He sidestepped out of sight. From behind, he murmured into her ear. "This will hurt. I'm sorry."

It was weird to hear but not feel the blows: ***THMMP BMMP FTTT POOMP!*** A billion burning needles leaped out of Holly's muscles! And a scream leaped out her mouth: "AAAHHHOOOOOOOWWWWW!"

Mmm, yes! Holly stretched like a cat to a wave of body-soothing warmth: "Ahhhh!" She claimed her brainy dark knight with a hug, he was hers, all hers! "If you really want to thank me, let me calculate tonight's date!"

Cal patted her back. "Yes, ma'am." He looked toward Chris Jobz, who was weeping over the unconscious Karate Queen. "Two Intellecta-pokes to his temples should restart his brain's arrogance lobes."

Holly couldn't resist. "Aw, you're not gonna kiss him?"

THE SURFVILLE CINEMA. THEATER SEVEN. 7:37 P.M.

Cal noted that Holly raised the armrest between them even though the upcoming movie was not romantic. And not exactly good cinema. He whispered, "I had planned to review the movie in theater four. *My Philosophical Autumn in Montegood Mansion.*"

Holly's knotting eyebrows telegraphed her repeated dislike of the "artsy-fartsy" movie genre. But Cal had to admit that in the past several weeks, she had educated him well about superhero movies. She whispered, "Review this instead. You haven't trashed a stinker in ages. Your readers love when you do that."

The movie title zoomed onscreen in towering bloody letters, accompanied by bombastic bass blurts: CREEPY CRAWLY COLOSSAL SPIDERS IV: THE SUCKENING!

This was illogical. Holly hated spiders. Last week, Cal and six super cops had barely held back a clawing, kicking, howling Holly after Tarantula Man had shot a quart of webbing into her beloved blond hair. Bennie the Rubber Cop told Cal that he'd never seen a perp beg to go to jail so fast.

Two teens—shirtless guy and ditzy girl—pranced onto the screen and into a dark forest. The ditz mewed, "Are there spiders out here? They're, like, totally icky!"

Cal sighed and mentally composed his review, his Intellacta-memory recording it for later transcribing. *Will dead teenager movies never die? Will idiot writers ever stop writing idiot scripts? This is a bad movie where it would NOT be more interesting to watch the actors having lunch, because the cheekbones are so impossibly high, the facial expressions so vapid, and the ditzy intellects so low—I'm not just talking about the actresses—that I suspect movie producers tossed bimbo dolls into the giant cauldron of bubbling DNA from which they scoop out the latest boy bands— HEY!*

A car-sized spider had leaped across the screen in all its slimy-fanged glory. Audience girls had squealed. And Holly had grabbed Cal's arm.

Cal looked at Holly. Holly looked at Cal. He calculated that he could swim for 3.7 hours in those big blue eyes.

Holly's smoky smile could have melted a glacier. She whispered, "Your turn to save the day." She kissed him and faced the screen. "Hold me."

Cal wrapped his critical crimefighter arm around Holly's super-strong, yet soft and supple shoulders. He continued his review. *But I can love a bad movie—*

Right on cue, cinematic spider fangs plunged into nubile teenage flesh. Holly flinched. Cal hugged her close. Holly nuzzled closer. Silky, strawberry-scented hair caressed Cal's face.

—when it is womansplained to me.

3 *KITTYGIRL IN:* THE FIENDISH BRAIN FREEZER!

SURFVILLE, CALIFORNIA. THE BACKYARD LOCATION OF THE OFFICIAL SUPER HOLLY HANSSON FAN CLUB MONTHLY MEETING. EARLY SEPTEMBER. A SATURDAY. 2:41 P.M.

"Careful, Kat," the villain taunted, "you're gonna rip it!"

Katsuko "Kittygirl" Kimura hotly glared up at her stepbrother Johnny, who held a comic book high over her head. Not just any comic book, it was the one that Super Holly Hansson had just written! But Kittygirl pulled in her claws, Johnny was right. With her cat superpowers, she was stronger and faster than a dozen teenage boys, and she could claw through steel, but Johnny still teased her right in front of the fangirls! She wiggled her hips and tippy-toed as she measured for a pounce, last time she'd overshot by twenty feet. A *"RAOWL!"* rumbled up her throat.

A **WHOOSH** made Kittygirl's ears perk up.

Girls bounced on rows of folding chairs. A few

leaped up and pointed. A few others floated up to see better. "Lookit!" "Up inna sky!" "It's a bird!" "It's a plane!" "It's a beautiful super writer!"

Johnny looked up to the sky with dreamy eyes. "It's her."

Kittygirl's heart jumped with joy. "It's Super Holly!"

VVVVOOOOOOSHHH!!! Out of the sunny sky meteored a tall blond woman in a blue, long-sleeved supersuit with a yellow up-arrow on the chest. Super Holly Hansson landed at Kittygirl's side— *THHHMP!*—and smiled at her fans. Holly stood so tall, hands on hips, red cape and long blond hair fluttering, so brave and pretty, she was the best of all the superheroes EVER!

Kittygirl looked down at her blue t-shirt with nothing on the chest. And no cape. Not till she grew up.

Fangirls clapped. "YAY!"

"Hi, Holly," Johnny sighed. He smiled up at Holly.

Holly smiled nicely down at Johnny. She took the comic book. "I mailed this to your little sister."

Johnny's eyes had gotten real big when Holly had touched his hand. He looked sheepishly at Kittygirl. "Sorry, Kat. I just wanted to say hi to Holly." He ran into the house and said over his shoulder, "Bye, Holly!"

Holly held up the comic book. "My faithful fangirls, I wrote my latest comic book about—"

DAH-DAH DUM DUM DUM, DAH DAH DA-DA-DA-DA DUM! A tinny version of Turkey in the Straw blared from the front of the house, drowning out Holly. Fangirls flew, super-speeded, but mostly stampeded out of the backyard and squealed, "Ice cream! Ice cream! Ice cream!"

A folding chair fell over: **KLUNK!** The other chairs stood empty. Holly and Kittygirl stood alone. Kittygirl's tummy sank. "Sorry, Holly. They all liked your story."

Holly put the comic book into her yellow hip purse and laughed. "I'll sign this for you. And it's okay. Even I, the mightiest superhero on Earth, can't compete with ice cream on a hot day." Her voice went all schoolteacher. "Now, how did Johnny sneak up and grab your comic book when you have super-kitty hearing?"

Kittygirl pouted. "I was reading your comic book to the fangirls, and I got so into it that he caught me off guard. I got mad and I extended my claws and fangs and I hissed at him. But he just laughed at me!"

Holly put a strong, comforting hand on Kittygirl's shoulder. "When I get really mad, steam blows out my nose."

"Wow! Bet that scares bad guys!" Kittygirl looked down at her feet. "I wish I could be scary."

A finger under Kittygirl's chin tipped her head up to look into Holly's big, blue eyes. "Sweetie, no thirteen year old boy is scared of his little sister, even when she has superpowers. You know Johnny loves you, right?"

He really did. Johnny always let Kittygirl sit with him and talk about school and friends and life. He always stuck up for her, although now that she didn't have to hide her kittycat powers anymore, he didn't have to do that so much. He always praised the stories she wrote, even though they were not anywhere near as good as Holly's. And he always asked when Holly was gonna stop by again. "Johnny's a great brother. I love him. And he really likes you."

"He's a good boy, but I'm twice his age." Holly scratched behind Kittygirl's ear, ooo that felt nice. "You're only eight. You'll be a great superhero when you grow up."

"Johnny says that too." Kittygirl looked up to her hero. Way up. Holly was six foot one. The sun behind Holly turned her blond hair into an angel halo. Kittygirl loved her own shiny black hair, but... wow. "Your hair's so pretty."

Holly knelt down and stroked Kittygirl's hair. "So's yours."

"Yeah, I like it." Kittygirl tossed her head to swish her long shiny black hair. That reminded her! "It bugs me that Sailor Luna has BLOND hair!"

Holly nodded. "The animators do that so we can tell the Luna girls apart."

Kittygirl stomped her foot. "But tall blond Japanese anime girls don't feel real!"

The corners of Holly's mouth drooped. "Sometimes, when I look in the mirror, I don't feel real either."

Kittygirl felt guilty. She squeezed Holly's hand. "I'm sorry, I forgot how your powers changed your looks. But even before, you were tall and brave and strong." She hung her head. "Not like me."

Holly put a finger under Kittygirl's chin and tipped her head up. Holly's loving smile overcame the fierceness of her beaky nose. "You've got the proportionate strength of a dozen kittycats!"

Kittygirl sighed. "You can punch through steel."

"You can claw through steel!"

"You can fly."

"You're kittycat fast!"

"You've got telekinesis. And super-strength."

"You always land on your feet! And you saved me once."

"You saved me first." Kittygirl remembered that fateful day when Holly got superpowers and blond hair, and had grown out of her Batman t-shirt real fast. Holly had been so heroic, Kittygirl had been so afraid.

Holly hugged Kittygirl and murmured in her ear. "I'd save the president of my fan club anytime, anywhere. And I have something else for you. But first, let's get ice cream. It was hot flying over here." Holly leaped over the house.

"Mom doesn't like that," Kittygirl said when they landed in the front yard. The fangirls were gathered near a white, shiny ice cream van the size of a school bus. Their snaky tongues licked and slurped, their happy mouths chomped and sang, a cool creamy chorus in Kittygirl's super-sensitive ears: "Mmm!" *SLUP! LAP! CHMMMP!* "Chocklit!" *LUP LUP LUP!* "Nilla!" *GULP!* "Yummy!"

One girl looked plaintively up at an open window in the van. "Do you have organic blueberry?"

A long, white-sleeved arm thrust out and handed her a blue ice cream cone. A happy, chilly voice: "Of c-c-c-course, little lady, it's f-f-f-free ice cream day!"

Holly tugged Kittygirl's hand. "C'mon!"

Kittygirl shook her head. "I'm lactose intolerant."

Holly suddenly looked so sad! Kittygirl squeezed Holly's hand again. "Don't worry, Mom keeps soy ice cream for me in the freezer! It's good!"

Mom trotted out of the house, an ice cream cone in her hand. She stood up to Holly. Mom was a foot shorter, but her accent sharpened her voice into a samurai sword. "Holly, I've told Katsuko! No JUMPING over the HOUSE!"

Holly seemed to shrink an inch. "Sorry."

Mom handed over the cone. "Here you go, Katsuko."

Kittygirl's nose twitched. Ooo, spicy! Was it... she took a tongue-tingling bite. "My favorite! Wasabi! Thanks, Mom!"

Holly wrinkled her nose. "Ew. I want strawberry." She walked to the open van window, her cape and blond hair fluttering, her long strong legs striding. Kittygirl had to take twice as many steps to keep up.

From the window poked a man's head with skin so pale that it made Holly's Swedish skin look tan. He smiled, showing long icicle teeth. His pointy nose put Holly's nose to shame, it would be at home on the wicked witch of the west. He handed Holly a cone, five pink scoops tall. "For our most p-p-p-powerful and b-b-b-beautiful hero!"

"Thanks," said Holly. She took a bite. Her eyes widened. "Mmm." Then a big bite. "MMM!" Then a bigger bite. ***"MMMMM!!!"*** Then a bunch of super bigger bites. She licked her lips and closed her eyes. "This is WONDERFUL!"

Holly looked happy. Kittygirl sidled up to the fangirls, she knew what would make Holly even happier. She got in front of the club treasurer, who gulped down the last little tip of an ice cream cone. "We need to tell Holly how we liked her comic book. Can you start?"

The girl licked her lips and nodded fast. "Yeah! I'll tell her it was so funny how the superheroine got mad and the bad guys were too dumb to stop getting her mad and... uh..." The girl frowned. "Ow."

Kittygirl cocked her head. "Are you okay?"

More fangirls sounded unhappy. They made sad faces and rubbed their heads and mewled like hungry kittens. "Ow!" "Ooo!" "Brain-freeze!" "Owee!" "It hurts!" "OWWWITCH!"

They all shut up. Their faces all went blank.

Kittygirl's heart thumped. "Girls? Hello?"

They just stood there.

Kittygirl leaped to her mom and shook her. "Mom?"

Mom's head wobbled, but otherwise she just stared into space.

Kittygirl's tummy got hot despite the soy ice cream inside it. "Holly! Something's wrong!" No answer. Slowly Kittygirl turned. OH NO!

"I... uh... ow." Super-strongest-of-them-all Holly Hansson swayed dizzily, her arms limp, her mouth open, her lips flecked with sticky pink. The tippy-tip end of her ice cream cone fell from her fingers. With a crisp crackle—*SSSKKKKKLLLKK!*—thick frost engulfed Holly's head from the ears on up, like her brain was super-cold ice. She stood still and stared into space. Just like mom. Holly's blank face and unblinking eyes made Kittygirl's spine feel cold.

Kittygirl grabbed Holly's hips and tried to shake her. "Holly? HOLLY!"

Holly didn't move, her smooth super legs were like two oak trees.

From the front and back of the ice cream van gushed walls of icy steam. That would hide the fangirls and Holly and her mom from the whole neighborhood! A door on the van opened. The ice cream guy's chilly voice came forth. "Meet me in my c-c-c-cool clubhouse, my f-f-f-frosty fanclub! HEH HEH HEH HEH HEH!"

That tinny music pierced Kittygirl's ears again. The fangirls, her mom, and Holly jerked to attention like wind-up toys. All together, they turned toward the van door, lined up, and began robot-marching into the van.

Hair fluffed up on the back of Kittygirl's neck. She swallowed a scaredy-cat wail that crawled up her throat. She looked left, right... the house! Call the cops! Kittygirl ran over the lawn, leaped up the steps to the front door...

WHUMP! And knocked Johnny on his butt. He sat up. "Oof! Kat, why—"

She jumped up and blurted it all in one breath! "Call the cops! Mom and Holly and the fangirls got brain frozen! That ice cream guy's gonna steal 'em!" She was so scared that she wanted to barf, but something else blurted out her mouth: "And I gotta try to stop him!"

Johnny gasped. "I'll phone!" He hugged Kittygirl. "You can do it, Kat!" He scrambled to his feet. Then his face got sour, like when Kittygirl played her Sailor Luna videos. He shook his head like he was dizzy. "Ow. What's with that stupid music?"

Kittygirl swallowed hard and whirled toward the van. Her heart hammered her ears and her feet clawed up hunks of front lawn as she ran faster, faster, FASTER! She leaped!

And landed feet-first behind Holly, who was the last one marching into the evil van. Kittygirl followed. Maybe if she imitated Holly's robotic walk, she could fool the bad guy. She did not sway her hips like Holly. Last week, in the privacy of her bedroom, Kittygirl had tried to imitate Holly's pretty sashay. And had knocked over her big tall bookshelf. Mom had made Dad bolt it to the wall after yelling, "It could have squished her!"

An icy breeze billowed past Holly's red cape, making Kittygirl blink. Inside, the fangirls and her mom were lined up and facing the tall skinny ice cream guy. He wore a long white coat, white pants, white cap, and white shoes, which matched his bone white face and toothy smile. Behind him was the van's driver seat, next to him was a big white freezer.

Holly stepped into line beside the fangirls, stood like a soldier, and stared at Ice Cream Guy. Kittygirl did the same. But her mind chased for ideas like a cat after a mouse. What did Holly do to bad guys? Punch them! Well, Kittygirl was strong. And if she knocked out the bad guy, maybe his slaves would wake up, that was how it worked in comic books. Kittygirl tensed for a pounce. "Rrr!"

Ice Cream Guy looked at her. "Hey!"

Kittycat quick, Kittygirl leaped! She swung her fist at a pointy chin. "ROWL!"

Even quicker, a bunch of nozzles poked out of the

walls and fired: ***BBBBBTTTHHHHHHHHHPPPPPPP!***

Kittygirl was covered neck to toes in a creamy cold clump that instantly froze hard as a rock. She squirmed and twisted! "MMMRRRROWL!" But all she could move was her head. The rest of her was getting cold, so cold.

Ice Cream Guy gloated down at her. "HEH HEH HEH HEH HEH! How do you like my ice cream guns, kitty cat?"

Kittygirl looked at her blond superheroine. "Holly, wake up! Please save me!"

Holly didn't look back. Ice Cream Guy ran a finger under Holly's chin. His teeth seemed to get sharper. "Sh-sh-sh-she cannot hear you! She is completely in my b-b-brain-freezing power! Just like her fangirls! And your mommy!" He turned to the open van door. "Ah, and one more! Come in, my latest ice cream minion!"

Johnny walked into the van. But why, he had just said he hated that ice cream song... oh no! In his pocket! An ice cream bar stick! And that dumb DUM DUM DUM song was still going. Kittygirl yelled at Ice Cream Guy, "Can't you turn that stupid music off?"

"No! I like traveling music!" Ice Cream Guy handed some keys to Mom and told her, "Drive to the police station."

Kittygirl yelled, "The police are gonna get you!"

The van lurched. Ice Cream Guy stumbled a moment. Mom was not so great at driving big cars.

Ice Cream Guy opened the big freezer. "No, I will get the cops!" He pulled out several little freezer bags with straps. "For mine is the power over all things ice cream! F-f-f-first, my ice cream brain-freezes my minions!" He began strapping the freezer bags to the fangirls. "Then I activate them with my icy m-m-m-music... wait." He stopped and looked suspiciously at Johnny.

Johnny stood next to Holly. He didn't even look at her.

Ice Cream Guy asked Johnny, "You didn't c-c-c-call the cops, did you?"

Kittygirl thought at Johnny, *Please say yes, please say yes, please say yes!*

"No, sir," Johnny said.

Ice Cream Guy continued strapping on freezer bags. "Excellent!"

Kittygirl's heart sank. She was so cold that her arm and leg muscles were sore. Her ice cream prison was so hard and tight that she couldn't even shiver.

Ice Cream Guy stood in front of the fangirls. Each one had a freezer bag on her chest. He waved his finger like a band director. "Girls, show me your sales pitch!"

The fangirls smiled like happy dollies and sang like birds in perfect tune: "Wanna have some ice cream?"

Ice Cream Guy grinned like his icy heart had thawed. "Adorable." He handed Johnny two small metal boxes. "After the fangirls feed my ice cream to the police, attach this receiver to the old air raid siren and the other to the emergency broadcast transmitter." He turned his long white face to Kittygirl, showing his merry eyes and mean smile. "I will blanket the air and the airwaves with my brain-freezy ballad!"

Did all supervillains blab their evil plans? Well, Kittygirl would blab something back! "You won't get away with this!"

Ice Cream Guy blinked. "But I'm doing that right now."

Kittygirl hung her head. She didn't even have a good catchphrase.

Ice Cream Guy leaned down into Kittygirl's face. His breath smelled tutti-fruity. "Why aren't you in my power?"

Kittygirl ran her tongue on her fangs and hoped his big nose would come into range.

Instead, Ice Cream Guy turned to Holly. "Keep an eye on Kittygirl."

Holly walked to Kittygirl, leaned down, and mushed her face on Kittygirl's shoulder. Holly's head felt so cold.

Ice Cream Guy snapped, "Not like that! Watch her and grab her if she gets loose."

Holly straightened up and stared down at Kittygirl.

The van stopped. The door opened. Kittygirl saw parked black and white cars outside.

Ice Cream Guy pointed at the door and his smile was big and toothy and happy and evil! "Go, my frosty songbirds! Turn the police into my obedient copsicles! HEH HEH HEH HEH HEH HEH!!!"

The fangirls marched past Kittygirl.

She pleaded at them, "No! Girls! Don't help the bad guy!"

They didn't look at her. They just smiled sweetly as they left the van.

Johnny marched by, carrying the metal box.

Kittygirl pleaded again: "Johnny? Please look at me!"

He didn't. Kittygirl's mom marched by. Ice Cream Guy strapped a freezer bag to her.

Kittygirl pleaded yet again. "Mom?"

Mom followed Johnny out of the van. Ice Cream Guy closed the door. He walked to the driver seat.

Holly was still standing near her. Kittygirl looked up at her poor, poor hero. "Holly. Please, please, please wake up."

Holly just stared with cold, blank eyes.

Kittygirl couldn't move. Except for the tear running down her cheek.

INSIDE A BIG WAREHOUSE. TEN MINUTES LATER.

Ice Cream Guy said, "Holly, put the c-c-c-cat out."

Holly picked up the big ice cream boulder encasing Kittygirl, marched out of the van, and put it down.

Kittygirl felt like she was turning into a snowgirl. Her fingers and toes tingled, going numb.

Ice Cream Guy walked up, leaned down, and laughed. "HEH HEH HEH HEH HEH! Hello, kitty cat! I need— YIPE!"

Kittygirl had snapped her sharp fangs, missing a long pointy nose by a whisker! ***"HISSSSS!"***

Ice Cream Guy had jumped back. He looked scared, but only for a few seconds. He smoothed out his white shirt. "Ahem! As I was saying, I want a helpless hero to whom I show off my icy plans. You will have to do. Super Holly isn't much of an audience right now."

Holly was a superwoman statue, at attention at Ice Cream Guy's side. Her forehead gleamed white with that horrible frost, which wasn't melting.

"Holly," Kittygirl said, "please beat up the bad guy!"

Holly's eyes were two empty, blue ice marbles.

"S-s-s-silly kitty," Ice Cream Guy chattered, "Super Holly hears no voice but mine! Observe! Holly," and Holly turned to him like a soldier facing a general, "from now on, smash anything that tries to h-h-h-harm me!" He smiled nastily at Kittygirl. "N-n-n-nip at me again and Holly will turn you into a Kittygirl p-p-p-pancake!"

Okay, Kittygirl would not attack Ice Cream Guy even if she got loose. But she could study his lair. She looked all around. Over her shoulder, the warehouse doorway was opening. A freezer big enough to hold an elephant was on one side of the warehouse. And on the other side was... the world's biggest empty ice cream cone? A forty-foot tall metal cone stood on its pointy end. It would take LOTS of ice cream to fill THAT! A control panel was about twenty feet from the cone. The panel had a big dial and buttons and knobs and blinky lights like those silly machines in those old black and white monster movies that made Kittygirl giggle. She did not feel like giggling now.

Ice cream trucks drove into the warehouse. Ice Cream Guy clapped. "Ah, r-r-r-right on time! Follow me, Holly!"

Holly robot-walked after Ice Cream Guy to the control panel. Even her hip swaying seemed stiff.

A shaft of sunlight shot through a window near the warehouse roof and onto Kittygirl's face. So nice and warm! Despite her fear and sadness, she purred.

The trucks stopped. Twelve blank-faced guys wearing white ice cream suits marched out. They lined up before Ice Cream Guy and Holly. Ice Cream Guy commanded them: "Ice cream minions! Report!"

One said in a dull, flat voice, "Television stations secure." Another said in a dull, flat voice, "Radio stations secure." And more and more dull and flat, for fire stations, football stadiums, and other stuff. Bad enough Kittygirl was freezing. She made an ugly face at the bad guy. "I'm already scared, now you wanna bore me too?"

Ice Cream Guy made an ugly face at Kittygirl. "Master plans are not b-b-b-boring!"

Kittygirl jutted out her jaw like Holly did sometimes. "Yours is!"

Ice Cream Guy pouted his lips. "No it isn't!"

Kittygirl bared her fangs, "Yes it is," and stuck out her tongue, "NNN!"

Ice Cream Guy stomped his feet. "No, no, no it ISN'T!" Then he looked surprised. He smiled at Kittygirl and nodded. "Well, well. You got me bantering when I should be gloating. Like this." He rubbed his hands together with glee. "My t-t-t-trapped superhero, nearly everyone in town has feasted upon my ice cream. Soon, my Cone of Doom will beam my frosty frequency everywhere in town! You will helplessly watch as I turn every b-b-b-brain in range into ob-b-b-bedient ice! HEH HEH HEH HEH HEH!"

Kittygirl purred hard to calm down and because the sun on her face still felt really nice... wait! She could feel her fingers again! But how, the ice cream was so cold... her purring! It warmed her up! She purred harder.

Ice Cream Guy turned to Holly and pointed to the

top of the empty cone. "Holly, fill my Cone."

Holly reached toward the freezer. Two giant blue transparent hands formed before her. That was Holly's super-telekinesis that let her grab and punch really big stuff. Holly motioned with her human hands like she was scooping something up. Her blue telekinetic hands motioned the same way: they flew to the freezer and scooped up an elephant-sized glob of ice cream. Those hands dropped the ice cream into the cone with a **PLOIP!**

Kittygirl purred harder. She was warmer. The ice cream was looser! She could squirm a little bit!

Ice Cream Guy hopped like a happy puppy. "Now, Holly, fill my ice cream with your super t-t-t-telekinetic p-p-p-POWER!"

Like a zombie, Holly pointed her arms at the top of the giant cone. Big blue beams of light streamed from her hands and into the huge scoop of ice cream. It began to glow.

Kittygirl throbbed with super-purring power. Her ice cream cage softened more.

Ice Cream Guy punched buttons on the control panel. On its dial, a pointer pointing left began to slowly tilt toward a big red dot at the far right. And that ice cream music blared from the cone, even louder than Johnny's boom box that always made Mom mad. The ice cream blob topping the giant cone lit up in time with each tinny note. Ice Cream Guy's smile lit up too. "My superpowered song resonates! Soon, it will f-f-f-freeze every brain in town! Then they'll build me an even bigger ice cream plant! I'll sell even more frosty treats! I'll brain freeze the entire

Seaside county! I'll sell sell sell and get RICH RICH RICH! HEH HEH HEH HEH HEH!"

Kittygirl felt stronger, hotter, and she thought the bad guy's plan was really stupid!

Holly stared unblinkingly at the giant ice cream blob as she streamed power into it. Her blue supersuit and red cape made her look like a sleepwalking Superman. Except Holly's costume had short pants, like the Overlady's from Holly's action-packed and sad graphic novel.

Ice Cream Guy stared all googly-eyed happy at Holly. "My mighty minion. My pretty popsicle. My creamy cone." He nuzzled up to Holly's ear and moaned, "You and I, we shall make b-b-b-beautiful sundaes together." And yuck, yuck, YUCK, his wormy tongue licked from Holly's cheek all the way up to her frozen forehead: *SAH-LUUURRRRP!*

Kittygirl folded her cat-sensitive ears, but that icky lick still made her go, "EEEWWWWW!"

Ice Cream Guy turned toward Kittygirl, but only halfway. His tongue was stuck on Holly's frozen head! His eyes bugged out, he flailed his arms, he pushed at Holly, but his tongue stayed glued. Stronger-than-steel Holly didn't budge a millimeter. "Stugg," Ice Cream Guy said, "I'B STUUUUUGGG!"

Kittygirl flexed her legs and YES! She leaped free of the ice cream! She was kinda gooey, but she dared not lick herself clean because lactose made her tummy hurt and that glacier glob topping the giant cone glowed like a sun! How could she stop it, it was so big and she was so small... and that great big cone stood on its teeny tiny tip, a tip attached to the floor by just a few bolts! That was so stupid, the cone could fall and squish someone! Kittygirl got on all fours—she was lots faster that way—and she charged like a cheetah!

Ice Cream Guy's head bounced like a basketball on Holly's skull, but his eyes and frantically shaking finger pointed at Kittygirl. "Iceth cweam minionth! APPACK!"

A dozen minions charged. The closest one dove right at Kittygirl.

Kittygirl lashed out her clawed hand with a *"ROWL!"*

The minion's pants fell down and tangled around his knees. He face-planted on the floor with a ***SPLAT!*** Kittygirl hopped over him in a single bound.

Two more minions aimed fat handguns at her, the gun barrels looked just like the nozzles that had sprayed her back in the van. But to Kittygirl's fast kittycat vision, the two minions moved underwater slow! She lanced out a clawed hand and foot.

The guns split in half. A whole bunch of ice cream plopped out. The two minions got stuck in a creamy puddle that froze their feet to the ground.

The remaining minions stormed at Kittygirl. She jumped at them! Her long black hair fluttered like a cape! And she retracted her claws, she shouldn't scratch those poor guys, they couldn't help it. With super-kitty strength, Kittygirl whirled her arms and legs like propeller blades and bashed her fists and feet on minion faces: ***BIFF BOP BAM POW BOFF KA-POWIE!***

The minions plopped to the ground like jelly bowling pins.

Kittygirl's heart beat hard and fast and heroic! She flying-leaped over the control panel, Ice Cream Guy, and Holly, and the dial pointer was almost touching the red dot! Kittygirl landed feet-first perfect at the base of the giant cone. She extended her front claws: **SKNNT!** She slashed at the cone's tip, her hands a clawed blur! Metal shreds flew like a snowstorm! She howled, ***"ROWRRR, HISSSSS!"***

"NOOOOO! SSSSTOOOOBB!" yelled Ice Cream Guy. "Hoollbb! Grbb hrbb, GRBB HRBB!"

No way Holly understood that babbling. But Holly kept beaming power.

A creaking metal scream: ***KKKRRRRRRRRRRRRCK!*** The cone tilted like a giant movie robot about to faint.

"Timber!" yelled Kittygirl. She jumped twenty feet out of the way.

Uh oh, the cone fell right at Ice Cream Guy and Holly. Holly punched it with her giant telekinetic fist: ***BLONNNGGG!*** The cone flew across the warehouse and clanged on the floor like a giant bell: ***DONNNNNNNNNGGGG!*** Holly pantomimed a fist hammer, and her giant blue fist smushed the cone flat: ***KRRRUNKCH!***

Kittygirl smiled, that was exactly how Ice Cream Guy had told Holly to protect him. Ha!

The big blob of super ice cream gushed onto the floor and melted: ***BLURP BLURP BLURP BLUUUURRRRRP SLUSHHHHHHH.***

Kittygirl stuck her tongue out at Ice Cream Guy: "NNNNN!" Then a bolt of fear made her meow.

Ice Cream Guy's tongue wasn't stuck on Holly's head anymore. He smacked his lips and said, "Ow."

And he yelled, "HOLLY! GRAB HER!"

Holly turned her blank gaze to Kittygirl. Kittygirl's tummy turned to ice. Holly raised her right arm and aimed.

Gotta get away, gotta get AWAY! Kittygirl looked frantically around. The sunlight, the window near the roof! Kittygirl ran and put all her strength into a desperate leap! The window rushed closer, CLOSER!

Blue, elephant-trunk thick fingers squeezily engulfed Kittygirl from her neck to her toes. The window was inches away, so close, so far. Kittygirl looked over her shoulder. A fifty-foot long transparent arm stretched from Holly's right arm, pointing at Kittygirl like a compass needle. Kittygirl squirmed, but Holly's blue King Kong fist held Kittygirl like a kitten. Holly reeled her in.

Ice Cream Guy knelt in the giant ice cream puddle. He looked about to cry. "My ice cream. My lovely ice cream." He got up. He stalked toward Kittygirl. His eyes were mean, his teeth were gritted. "You did this!"

Kittygirl begged at the beautiful superwoman just a few feet away who was not coming to her rescue. "Holly! Fight that brain freeze! He's a mean bully and you're my hero and I love you!"

Holly did not wink, did not blink. She stood still, her telekinetic hand held Kittygirl so much super-stronger than that rock-hard ice cream prison. Holly's face was emptier than a Super Holly Hansson doll. At least those dolls smiled. Holly had been mad that those dolls had cute little noses instead of Holly's fierce eagle beak.

Ice Cream Guy shoved his skull-pale face into

Kittygirl's and barked tutti-frutti breath, "How many times must I t-t-t-tell you, Holly only listens to MY voice!"

Kittygirl wanted to nip his icicle nose, except Holly would defend him. Instead she thrust out her chin and yelled back, "Your breath stinks!"

Ice Cream Guy snorted. He walked into an ice cream truck and emerged with a small container of ice cream. "You are the only one who knows my icy plans. So I'll just freeze-dry your memory."

Kittygirl bared her fangs. "*ROWL!* Your ice cream won't work on me! I'm lactose intolerant!" Oh no! She cringed, she shut her mouth, but it was too late! Heroes weren't supposed to tell bad guys their weaknesses!

Ice Cream Guy smiled so big that his head looked ready to split. "Ah! Thank you!" He waved his hand over the ice cream container. Then he pulled a spoon out of his pocket and dug out a big cold fleshy-pink gob. "Have a little soy ice cream, kitty cat!"

Kittygirl locked her jaw and stiffened her lips. "No!"

Ice Cream Guy waved the spoon under Kittygirl's nose. "Are you sure?"

"I... I..." Kittygirl sniffed, and sniffed again. Her nose followed the spoon like a charmed snake. Her heart fluttered. She tried not to drool... *DRIP!* Oops. She breathed, "What flavor is that?"

Ice Cream Guy held the spoon real close to Kittygirl's trembling lips. "The most succulent, delicious, freshest tuna in the world, spiced with catnip! No kittycat can resist!"

That luscious scent snaked up Kittygirl's nose and

petted her brain. Her mouth opened... she shut it! Her nose twitched like a super-speed rabbit's. That smell, that SMELL!

Ice Cream Guy's teeth chattered as he laughed. "HEH HEH HEH HEH HEH! Your little head will soon be as empty as a ping-pong ball! Then I'll get away with Holly, and my next icy plan will not fail!"

Kittygirl pulled her head back, but only a little because Holly's huge transparent hand wrapped her body up as tight as a tiny hot dog in a super-strong bun. "No! You'll lose! Just like in good comic books!"

Ice Cream Guy's smile turned upside down. "Comic books? Who reads that g-g-g-garbage?"

Holly's right eye twitched at that G-word. But how... of course! Holly heard only Ice Cream Guy's voice! And if Holly got steaming mad... Kittygirl stared her fiery feline defiance into the bad guy's beady eyes. "Comic books are good! They make me laugh and cry!"

Ice Cream Guy held that tantalizing tuna treat so close and **SNIFF, SNNNNIFFF, DROOL,** Kittygirl wanted just one little taste so bad! He sneered at her. "Me too! When I see a little kid reading a c-c-c-comic book, I tear it up! I laugh, kid cries!" He pulled a comic book out of Holly's hip purse, held it in front of Kittygirl's face, and ripped it up. "Like this! HEH HEH HEH HEH HEH!"

Holly blinked. A drop of water ran down her frosty forehead.

Kittygirl hoped hard and yelled fast, being careful to not open her lips much or that evil spoon would get in. "Holly wrote that! And she wrote *The Last Super* graphic novel where the Overlady gave her life to save the world even though the world hated her! And I cried!"

"R-r-r-really?" Ice Cream Guy's frosty white eyebrows went up. He smooshed the spoon right onto Kittygirl's lips! "Sounds more like Last S-s-s-sucker!"

SLURP! Kittygirl's tongue had snaked out and she sucked it back in too late! A dab of that ice cream was in her mouth. So delicious... so hungry... her tummy rumbled.

Fat melted water drops rivered down Holly's face. Her lips skinned back from clenched teeth. She blinked.

Wake up, Holly, PLEASE WAKE UP! With the last of her strength, Kittygirl snarled, "*The Last Super* made me cheer and made me cry and taught me about being a hero and never being a meanie like you—" **GLUB!** *OH NO!* He'd shoved the spoon in her mouth!

Kittygirl's throat was opening up, her stomach was crawling up to that yummy ice cream! Kittygirl tried to spit, her mouth wouldn't obey! That taste, so meaty flaky rich, it swam around her tongue, her mind, her soul... *no, don't swallow, don't...*

Ice Cream Guy's pale face twitched as he yelled so close that his fruity breath blew tears off Kittygirl's face. "Swallow, kittycat! And while you're at it, swallow your stupid love of Holly's stupid comic books, no one needs a stupid story about a stupid woman throwing away her stupid life to save a stupid world, but so much stupid could only come from the stupid mind of— **GLUK!**"

The telekinetic hand holding Kittygirl vanished. She

landed on her feet. And for a moment, Kittygirl's heart sang even louder than her tummy growled.

Super Holly Hansson held Ice Cream Guy by the throat, hoisting him so high that the toes of his white shoes dangled a foot off the floor. Steam firehosed out Holly's nose, that looked so cool! And Holly looked so mad! She blasted her words like cannon balls, "NEVER! INSULT!! MY!!! WRITING!!!!"

Ice Cream Guy wet his pants. Kittygirl's nose shriveled at that smell.

Holly looked around like she was lost. "Where am I?"

Kittygirl blubbered around her mouthful of ice cream. "HOBBEE! Eve-oh eyefff cweam! I'b gubba swoww wit! *HELLLLB!*"

Holly turned to Kittygirl, and Holly's blue eyes got so big and loving and worried! Holly flicked a finger under Ice Cream Guy's chin—*TOK!*—and dropped his unconscious body like a sack of wet cement. She rushed up and knelt down and pinched Kittygirl's cheeks and said, "Spit it out, sweetie! Spit it out! Spit! SPIT!"

Kittygirl's tongue trembled, her throat opened... then she dived into Holly's eyes and found the strength to *PAH-TOO!*

Oops. "Sorry, Holly."

Holly wiped melty ice cream out of her eyes. A creamy blob skied down her big nose. "It's okay, sweetie." She stood up, a blue and blond skyscraper, the prettiest Superman ever! "Now wait while I call the police."

Kittygirl remembered! The fangirls! "Holly! The

cops are brain frozen too! Ice Cream Guy made the fan club do that!"

Holly's eyes got big and kinda scared. "Don't move!" She frantically tapped on her e-bracelet, big and shiny and golden just like Wonder Woman's but Holly's bracelet had a super smart phone built into it. Kittygirl wanted one of those.

"C'mon, c'mon," Holly mumbled, tapping her fingers on her wrist.

A little hologram appeared above the phone: a policeman with grey hair, wrinkles, and a frowny face. "Yeah?"

Holly blurted, "BENNIE! ARE YOU OKAY?"

The cop winced. "We're okay, kid, not so loud! Cute little girls gave us ice cream, then suddenly we all woke up with ice cream headaches." He sipped from a dingy mug. "Coffee helps."

Holly breathed a big sigh of relief. "Thanks goodness. Have the little girls drink something hot."

The cop raised an eyebrow and glanced at his mug.

Holly's face squinched. "Not cop coffee! Ew!" She poked her bracelet again. "Here's my location, send some cops. I have a nasty popsicle to toss into the cooler."

The cop smiled, tired but happy. "Sure, kid. Can't wait to read the paperwork on this one. Bye." The hologram vanished.

Holly petted Kittygirl's head. "Looks like all the brains thawed out when I knocked out the bad guy." She looked at Kittygirl with sad eyes. "Sweetie, you'll have to help me with that boring paperwork. I don't remember anything after I ate that strawberry ice cream."

Kittygirl raised her head into that soothing petting. "Anything for you, Holly."

The pile of minions moaned and groaned and wobbled to their feet. Holly warned them, "Boys, don't run," she picked up an ice cream van and pumped it like a barbell, "or you'll be playing with the big girls!"

Minions looked at Holly like she was the boss. One of them said, "No problem, Holly, we're on your side! That Ice Cream Guy brain froze us!" He cocked his head. He took out his wallet, pulled slips of paper from it, and glared at them. "And that cheapskate paid us in ice cream vouchers!"

Those guys had bruises and black eyes and spilt lips and torn white uniforms. Kittygirl felt guilty. "Guys? I'm sorry I beat you up."

They stopped rubbing their jaws and pulling up their ripped pants. They looked at Kittygirl, their faces the same as when they looked at Holly. "You did this? You're a tough little girl!"

"I guess go." Kittygirl looked up to her hero. "But I can't wait to be a hero like... Holly?"

Holly's eyebrows mooshed together into a frown. She rubbed her temples. "Ouch. Ow!"

Kittygirl's heart scaredy-cat pounded! "Is your brain freezing again? Please don't be mind controlled again!"

"No, that's all gone." Holly winced. "It's just that... *ow*... when your head is super-frozen and then thaws out fast, it really hurts." She gritted her teeth. "***Sssss***. Feels like... ***mnnnn***... a glacier is cracking my skull. From the inside." Holly's face looked like Mom's did when she had caught Kittygirl sharpening her claws on the wicker chair. Holly stared off to one side. Her lips were stiff, but angry words still came out. "Ffff, fudge! Darny warny! Shhh, shoot! Frak! Peaches!" She closed her eyes. Tears squeezed out. "OUCHIE!"

Mom switched to Japanese when she said bad words. Holly couldn't do that. Kittygirl swallowed a lump in her throat. Maybe she could help. She leaped up and wrapped her arms around Holly's neck. "You need a hug."

Holly's shoulders and neck were stiff as steel. She grumbled, "You're kind of sticky, sweetie."

Kittygirl purred, purred, purred. Strong and loud, deep and warm. Kittygirl rubbed her cheek on Holly's shiny blond hair. It smelled like strawberries. Kittygirl wanted Holly's shampoo.

Kittygirl felt Holly's muscles relax. Holly sounded happy and kind of sleepy: "Ohhhh. Mmm. That feels... *SIGH!*... really nice."

"Are you okay now?" said Kittygirl. She shifted to see Holly's face. Then she giggled, she couldn't help it!

Holly's smile was goofy and her eyes were crossed! She chirped like a birdie, "Yes, mommy!"

Wow. Kittygirl could make the mighty Holly act silly. With great purring, there also came great responsibility. She stopped.

Holly shook her head. "My headache's gone." She kissed Kittygirl. "For the world's cutest and most powerful heating pad."

"That's so sweet! *SNIFF!*" That was a minion.

Holly smiled at Kittygirl. Kittygirl smiled back. They smiled at the minions, who were aiming their phone cameras. Holly said, "Can you take some pictures of me and my hero?"

Kittygirl said, "Really?"

Holly said, "Really. Now hold still." She reached into her yellow hip purse and pulled out... a cape! A red cape just like Holly's! She tied it onto Kittygirl. "For my brave little hero." She knelt down, put her strong arm around Kittygirl's shoulder, and faced the cameras. "Now let's say cheese."

Minions took photos. One of them sniffed. "Dang it, I think I'm gonna cry."

Wow. Kittygirl wanted some of those pictures.

4 THE DIMENSIONAL DOLLAR!

This story was previously printed in Series 1963 A, An Anthology of California Writers, from the South Bay Branch of the California Writers Club. This is the first story I wrote starring—by popular demand—my rather Trumpy supervillain.

SEASIDE CITY, CALIFORNIA. THE SHRUB INTERNATIONAL SUPER DUPER BANK. MID-NOVEMBER. A FRIDAY. 3:52 P.M.

In comic books, Superman's human-size hands carried battleships like he was a super-mouse whose teeny-tiny paws perfectly balanced a pickup truck. In the real world, Super Holly Hansson also had super-strength, but she always thanked her giant-size telekinetic hands when she caught a falling school bus or juggled army tanks. Or in this case, slowly flew through a castle gate of a bank entrance while she carried a showboating Shrub and his riches without spilling a drop.

Holy waste the wealth, Holly thought as she

74

maintained her weightlifting pantomime, *I am NOT opening a checking account here!* The cavernous bank lobby boasted gold-plated walls, mahogany desks, employees in money-green spandex and capes—*civilians shouldn't wear capes!*—and marble superhero statues. Holly didn't like the button nose and bimbo smile on hers.

Robert Reech, host of *Rolling in Ritzy Riches*, strode up with his golden microphone and smarmy English accent. "Caviar riches and diamond dreams! Golden-blond Super Holly Hansson, the world's mightiest superhero, carries over her head with the greatest of ease Bankee Shrub, who sits his silver throne at his golden desk! Just look at those diamond and ruby studded desk drawers, what wonders might they contain?"

Holly wondered why she hadn't made Bankee cough up more than a $200,000 donation to Surfville Elementary School for her superpowered courier duty. One-percenters made her bulletproof skin crawl.

So did Bankee's Texland twang. "Hee hee hee! Howdy, Mr. Reech! I figgered mah new bank needed a lil' old deposit on opening day! Hee hee hee!"

Holly set the desk and throne down and looked up, right into Reech's TV cameras. Those pervy paparazzi zoomed their telephoto lenses, and Holly clenched her jaw at the thought of the six o'clock news anchor-moron leeringly televising a close-up of her yellow up-arrow chest logo... no, every camera was drawn to Bankee like a magnet, following the money! Even the camerawoman whose dress was tugged by a piping little girl: "Lookit, mommy! It's Super Holly, eh?"

Bankee reached into a desk drawer, got off his throne, and moseyed up to Holly's side. Tanned as a leathery cowboy, brownish grey hair, squinty and gleeful eyes, money-green three piece suit and cowboy hat, white silk shirt, and bolo tie with a doorknob of a diamond clasp, Bankee held a thick stack of bills which he riffled with his thumb: *FFFTT! FFFTT! FFFTT!* "Hee hee hee! See this here pocket change? One hundred of these one million dollar bills! Had the Shrub mint print 'em just fer today!" *FFFTT! FFFTT! FFFTT!*

Reech sniffed the stack with a smile. "Ah, smell the wealth!"

Holly sneered at the smell of greed.

With a "Hup! Hup! Hup! Hup! Hup," twenty guards in green armor, cowboy hat helmets, and holstered golden guns clank-clank-clanked up to the Shrub. And they fidgeted, had to be sweaty in there! Holly was grateful for her blue, soft, comfy supersuit— *Erg, except when it rides up!* She reached under her red cape, tugged, and wished working stiffs had better tailors.

The bank vault door looked fifteen feet tall and who knew how thick? Even that superpowered knuckle-dragger Harry Headbutt would take a minute to, as he'd say, "SMUSH STUPID DOOR!" Near the vault, a lady in a grey pantsuit showed a dollar to Cal "The Intellectual" Critbert. Cal wore his deliciously dark cape, cowl, and six-pack-abs body armor. He'd promised Holly that after he checked bank security, they'd have dinner, then an ocean sunset, then the latest Batman movie. Holly hadn't told Cal that she'd pick back row seats where she'd teach him for a change: super-smooching! Now Cal scanned that bill with his Intellecta-phone like it was currency from Mars. What was so special about one thin dollar?

Bankee's smirk turned Holly's stomach. "Thanks fer yer hep! Now git along, lil' filly!" *SLAP!*

Holly snorted steam out her nose as Bankee hoofed toward the TV cameras. He'd SLAPPED her! On the BUTT! *I'm a woman, not a horse... No! I'm a BUCKING BRONCO!* She reared up to her full six-foot-one, menacingly trotted toward that concocted cowboy, cocked her fist, took deadly aim—

Cal's grim, on-the-crimefighting-job voice shivered a thrill up Holly's spine. "Holly, come here! Now!"

She pouted and flew to her boyfriend. "I wasn't really gonna nail him into the floor." *Not all the way.*

Cal got into Holly's face quick as a flash. "Forget the Shrub! The bank's counterfeit expert asked me if this bill was a 3-D fake. It's not!" He shoved it before her eyes. "See? No holochip!"

Holly looked at it. "A one dollar bill. No hologram. So?"

The bank lady said, "Miss Hansson, look at George."

Holy frowny face! George Washington was not full-tooth smiling! Holly asked, "It's a bad counterfeit?"

Cal's big brown eyes danced in his scary black cowl. "No! It is far, far more! Its molecular vibrational frequency is not native to our world! This dollar is from another dimension! Do you know what that means?"

Yes, YES! Holly's heart triple-somersaulted! "It's a clue!" She grabbed Cal's shoulders, her soulmate connection to Cal preventing her super-strength from pulverizing him. "To finding my mommy!"

Her mommy and daddy. Fallen through a dimension rift when Holly was five years old. The no-parents superhero cliché that had hurt Holly's heart for twenty years. Holly drank the sight of that wonderful, hopeful dollar!

And Cal's yummy crooked smile. "Given time, I'll open dimensional rifts with this."

From behind came Bankee Shrub's shriek: "Hep! Hep me! He's got mah munny!"

Holly groaned and turned around. *Who took the candy from the baby?*

A guard riffled a stack of bills. He'd removed his helmet. Fiftyish male, greedy gleam in his beady eyes, his big face proudly broadcasting a smug smile, and orange hair piled in a poofy comb-over. "Dat's MY money, yuh LOOOOSER!" His foghorn voice was D-instead-of-TH tough guy after a six-pack. "Cashing out my mini-casino wuz a yummy snack. Now I, Billington Stumpfinger, will gorge on even plumper leaves of lettuce!" He put one of the million dollar bills to his lips and—*Holy cash flow!*—it slid into his mouth with the sound of a dollar into a snack machine: ***BVVT!***

Bankee Shrub's lips writhed in horror. "He ate mah million!"

Holly pressed her lips together to keep from laughing.

Armored guards piled on the cash-consuming villain. "Hup! Hup! Hup! Hup! Hup!" ***CLANG! CLANG! CLANG! CLANG! CLANG!***

"Yer fired!" bellowed Stumpfinger. He swept his

arms. About twenty times normal strength, Holly judged by how far he tossed the guards. Not so tough. He smacked his lips, said "Greed tastes good," and sucked in more bills: ***BVVT! BVVT! BVVT! BVVT! BVVT!***

In high school, Holly had protected geeks, nerds, fanboys, and fangirls from bullies. Now she had to protect the rich and whiny. She flew to Stumpfinger and grabbed his wrist. "Time you went on a diet."

Stumpfinger didn't drop the cash. He clamped his hand onto Holly's arm—"I'm still hungry!"—and tossed her like she was a doll. *How'd he get so strong?*

The bank lobby tumbled. A desk smacked Holly's back: "OOF!"

A green-clad employee smiled at her. "Need a low-starting-interest loan?"

Holly leaped to her feet. "No! Got any vitamins?"

FWHOOSH! How Holly loved the sound of Cal's black cape billowing! He'd rushed to her side and nodded at her. Holly nodded back. *Your turn!*

Cal drew his black, shiny, all-purpose Intellecta-gun, and ***BAH-KOOM!*** A Harry-Headbutt-stunning shell, Cal meant business!

"Ow!" Stumpfinger flexed his empty, unscathed hand. "Dat stung a little... my money." He sniffed to and fro like a hungry pit bull stalking a tasty house cat. "Where's my MONEY?"

The little girl held a stack of bills up to her mom. "Lookit, I putted this money with my money, eh?"

Stumpfinger stomped over and tore the cash from tiny, trembling hands. "Gimme dat!"

Holly would have torn over and taken out the trash,

except Cal grabbed her shoulder. "He's too strong," he whispered. "Let me find a weakness."

Stumpfinger's hands blurred faster and faster as he sucked in bills like a candy machine with a black hole motor: *BVVT-BVVT-VVT-VVT-VTT-VT-VT-VT-VT-VT-* "EEE-YUCK!!!"

He pulled a bill out of his sour mouth and tore it to bits. "A Canadian dollah. Poison."

The quivering little girl hugged her trembling mommy. "You're scaring me, eh."

Stumpfinger towered over the cringing duo. *Was he... yes, he was several inches taller!* He raised his fist like a caveman club. "Puny immigrant. Bankrupt me, will yuh?"

That slimy BULLY! Holly flung off her boyfriend's hand and flew at Stumpfinger, forming a transparent, blue, bowling ball of justice around her right fist! "I'm cashing you out!"

Cal shouted, "Holly! No!"

No, Holly HIT! She plowed her telekinetic fist onto Stumpfinger's kisser: *BOMP!*

What th'?!?! Stumpfinger hadn't moved, not even a hairsbreadth! He smiled, teeth gleaming like pearls. "Here's yer change!"

His short-fingered fist zoomed faster than a speeding bullet.

THOOOOOOOMMMKRNNNCH!!! Holly hurled backwards and her brain ricocheted in her skull and she hoped her eagle beaky nose wasn't bouncing in there with it and a nuclear migraine exploded in her face and tidal-waved her head and her ears rang like church bells and she'd never been hit so HARD—

KKKKLLLLLLLLLLLOOOOOOOOOOOOOOOONNNNNNNG GGGGGGGGG!!!!!

Ow. Okay. Being embedded three feet into a giant bank vault door ran a close second. Holly had punched through thick steel before, but her fist had never hurt like her super-aching vertebrae. And grating ribs. And sore skull. And dislocated shoulder. And soon-to-be black and blue butt.

Cal hung his head.

The little girl whimpered.

Bankee Shrub asked the dumb question of the century. "Miss Hansson! Are yew okay?"

"Yeah," Holly wheezed with aching lungs. "Fortunately your nice, soft, super-steel vault door cushioned my landing."

Owowowowowow. Felt like a doctor was welding Holly's ribs with a blowtorch. Super-healing was kicking in. She grabbed the edges of her steely crater and pulled. *Owowowowowow—*

POP! She spilled onto the floor. *Ow.* She grabbed her right wrist and yanked. Her dislocated arm slipped back into its socket with another **POP!** *Ow.*

Cal knelt before her and scanned with his Intellecta-phone. His big brown eyes filled with her pain. He hissed, "You're healing efficiently! Stay down, I have a theory!"

He put a holochip on the other-dimensional dollar. The bill shimmered. George Washington morphed into Ronald Reagan. The denomination, Holly had never seen so many zeroes!

Cal whispered, "I'm sorry."

Holly blinked. *Why would Cal say that?*

BVVT! The last million-dollar bill slid into Stumpfinger's mouth. He was eight feet tall. Massive muscles burst off his guard armor, revealing green spandex with a dollar sign chest logo. *How original.* He howled to the heavens, "Look at me! I'm—*BURRRRRP!*—HUUUUUUGE!"

Bankee, Reech, and the bank employees cowered behind mahogany desks. TV cameras peeked around superhero statues. Recovering guards aimed guns. *BANG! BANG! BANG! BANG! BANG! BANG! BANG!*

Stumpfinger wasn't even scratched. "Puny ninety-nine-point-nine-percenters! I'm superpowered to duh tune of one hunnert million, four hunnert tousand, two hunnert and seventy six dollahs!" He rose to hover midair. "Duh greater duh denomination—"

Cal strode toward the villain. "The greater your superpower."

Stumpfinger puffed out his macho chest. "Stealing my lines, Poindexter?"

"I'm wondering if you're full yet." Cal's black-caped back was to Holly, but she could almost hear his massive mind calculating the villain's defeat. He held the dollar in plain view at his side, like he'd forgotten it. But Cal never forgot anything...

Realization smacked Holly in her fast-healing face. If a Canadian dollar meant bankruptcy, an other-dimensional dollar... which could find her mommy! Holly's breaking heart hurt more than her knitting ribs.

Stumpfinger stroked his chin and dropped his "th" again. "I'm tinking about dessert."

Cal flicked the dollar like a fishing lure. "You don't

want this. Way too rich."

That money moron licked his lips and still did not notice the bait! "I'll gobble at duh Shrub mint."

Holly's Batboy needed help. She put the back of her hand to her forehead, bent her legs, arched her back like the beaten yet sexy superheroines in way too many comic books, and wailed like an overacting opera singer, "Ow! I'm hurt and helpless! The pain, the horrible, unbearable, wretched pain! Won't my handsome hero comfort me?"

Yes! Every eye turned to her, she'd have to try that at her next open mic! Cal dashed to her, his dollar-clutching hand behind him for the villain to plainly see. "My poor, pretty, damsel in distress!" He knelt before her, kissed her, and whispered, "I love you."

Holly kissed him back. "I love you more."

Greed throbbed Stumpfinger's voice. "What's dat yer holding?"

Cal stood up and faced the villain. "Nothing."

Stumpfinger stomped toward Cal. "Gimme dat."

Cal backed away. "No! You shall not have it— URG!"

It took every iota of Holly's willpower to stay still. Stumpfinger had grabbed Cal by the throat and held him high.

Cal held out the bill and choked, "Here!"

"Tanks!" Stumpfinger flicked his wrist.

Cal flew twenty feet, bounced off a desk, and sprawled with a horrible limpness... and winked at Holly! He could take a fall, he was Holly's sparring partner!

Stumpfinger held the bill overhead like Aladdin beholding the magic lamp. "Wuh, wuh, one. Trillion.

Dollahs. Ohhhh..." He drooled.

Holly pouted. *C'mon, eat it!*

Stumpfinger sniffed the bill. He crowed, "And now, I will become..."

Holly winced. *Please don't say it.*

"...like unto a GOD!" *He said it. Jerk.*

Cal's plan and Holly's hope slid into hungry lips: ***BVVVVVV—***

Stumpfinger's smile turned upside-down.

The bill stopped. Shimmered. Went back to one dollar. And began sliding out: ***VVVVVB—***

NO! Holly flew at Stumpfinger! Clamped her legs and left arm around him! Shoved her right palm onto that gluttonous mouth! And yelled, "EAT IT! EAT THAT DOLLAR, YOU GREEDY, OVERSTUFFED, CORRUPT CASH MACHINE! EEEEEEEAT IT!"

Stumpfinger punched and pawed and sputtered, "Bfft! Mmmph! Umph! Nooofff!"

The bill slid in, out, in, out: ***BVVV! VVVB! BVVV! VVVB!***

Holly howled, "YOU WON'T..." *Oof! Ow!* "...GET RID OF ME!" She hugged harder, harder, HARDER, her smooshing super-bosom was gonna be super-sore and she DIDN'T CARE! Stumpfinger couldn't land direct punches, just glancing cannonball blows. *OUCH, another broken rib, doesn't he know that hugging in boxing means take a breather?*

The little girl hopped and clapped. "Get him, Holly!"

Holly pushed harder on that writhing face. Stumpfinger ran and slammed her into a wall: ***WHUMP!*** Then the vault door: ***CLANG!*** Then the Super Holly statue: ***CLUNK!*** Its severed stone head rolled on the floor to sweetly smile up at Holly.

A bank guard moaned, "I've dreamed of Holly hugging me like that."

Holly rolled her eyes. *Oh, brother.*

Stumpfinger grabbed Holly's wrist. And SQUEEZED!

"OOOOWWWWWWW!!!" Holly's forearm exploded with pain and crackled like popcorn!

That thin hope of finding Holly's mommy began sliding out of Stumpfinger's grin. But Holly knew her duty. She channeled all her superpower into her forehead and headbutted a blue telekinetic sledgehammer onto Stumpfinger's big fat mouth: ***BDOOOOOOOOOOOOOMMM!!!***

Holly stood, right arm limp and throbbing. Her ribs were burning shrapnel, her knees melting butter. But Stumpfinger's pout as the last tip of the dollar crept into his mouth made her smile.

Stumpfinger swayed. "No." He went cross-eyed. "Wanna build walls." His mammoth muscles melted. "Wanna stay rich." He shrank to normal. "Don't wanna be..." He gagged, opening his mouth with a cash register ***CHA-CHING!*** A stack of bills jumped out and onto the floor. "...a bankrupt..." His comb-over fell off, revealing shiny dome. "...loser."

Holly flicked a finger under Stumpfinger's chin: ***TOK!*** He fell on the marble floor with a spread-eagle, satisfying ***SPLAT!***

FWHOOSH! Cal rushed past her, frantically searched the pile of bills, and grabbed the dollar. "I have it... oh no!"

The dollar was glowing.

Cal dropped it and stepped back. It vanished in a

flash of light.

Holly stared at the patch of floor where the dollar had been, and now was not; where just beyond, maybe her mommy was waiting for her. *I'm not gonna cry. I will NOT cry...* A warm tear crawled down her cheek. *Nuts.*

Cal cradled Holly in comforting arms and inky cape. "I'm so sorry. The exposure to Stumpfinger's tremendous superpower increased the dollar's molecular vibrational frequency, sending it back to its home dimension." He patted Holly's back. "How do you feel?"

Her healing ribs, arm, and nose throbbed. *Ow.*

Bankee Shrub knelt over semi-digested millions. "Mah munny. Mah poor munny. SOB!" *Hee hee!*

The mother and the little girl hugged. "I love you, mommy. Can we meet Holly now, eh?"

Another warm tear. "I feel poor, Cal. I feel poor."

5 THE INTELLECTA-RHAPSODY!

(I read all the parts and did all the sound effects for this story myself when I received the 2017 audio story award at the San Mateo County Fair Literary Contest. I also used some royalty free music. If you want to perform my story with a cast, here it is in script form.)

Narrator (can be Super Holly because this is from her point of view): For Bugs Bunny, for Woody Woodpecker, and for Tom & Jerry, who have all danced to this tune. (PAUSE) The shoulder of Highway 101 south. Thirty miles north of Seaside City. A Saturday. 11:32 A.M.

Music: The Hungarian Rhapsody.

Super Holly: Not again!

Narrator: whined Super Holly Hansson.

Narrator: KER-POW! went the ray-gun barrel

poking out of the Intellecta-car's dashboard.

Super Holly: OWWWITCH!

Narrator: Holly's mighty superheroine face burned and itched and twitched... and her beloved blond hair was smoking! So this was how Daffy Duck's face felt if Elmer Fudd's shotgun was from the planet Krypton! She jerked her fist out of the sparking hole she'd punched into the dashboard and growled,

Super Holly: You started it!

Intellecta-car: NEGATIVE.

Narrator: The Intellecta-car monotoned.

Intellecta-car: YOU MADE IMPROPER GESTURES.

Narrator: The dashboard's morphing displays and glowing buttons coldly glared. How did her boyfriend Cal kept track of them when he drove this obnoxious car? Holly crossed her arms and slammed back into the driver seat, no longer caring how its black, leathery kevlar deliciously caressed her thighs.

Super Holly: I was PANTOMIMING! How else do I drive you when you don't have a steering wheel, or gas or brake pedals?

Intellecta-car: INPUT CORRECT COMMAND CODES.

Super Holly: My powers are flight, super-strength, and super-telekinesis. Not carburetor telepathy!

Narrator: From the passenger seat, Cal "The Intellectual" Critbert spoke spine-tingling grim.

Cal (Batman-esque grim): Holly Hansson.

Narrator: So formal. Cal must be angry. But not half as angry as Holly was! She faced her caped and cowled boyfriend.

Super Holly: WHAT?!?!

Narrator: Cal tap-tap-tapped a fingertip on his black-armored temple.

Cal: You damaged my car's telepathy circuit. Intellecta-car! Estimated self-repair time!

Intellecta-car: 39 MINUTES, 17 SECONDS.

Narrator: Holly snapped,

Super Holly: How long to repair your manners?

Intellecta-car: MANNERS CIRCUITS UNDAMAGED. YOUR MANNERS ARE IMPERFECT.

Narrator: Cal spoke in that lofty, oh-so-patient teacher tone that Holly oh-so-hated.

Cal: You insisted on this. You wanted to drive, as you said, 'your dark and smart Intellecta-Batmobile.'

Super Holly: Stay out of this!

Narrator: Yelled Holly, slamming her fist down for emphasis. All in an instant! The car roof opened! The passenger seat rocketed skyward! Cal yelled,

Cal: HOLLEEEEeeeeeeee...

Narrator: Up, up, and far away, a parachute opened. Holly lifted her fist to reveal a big red button.

Super Holly: Why didn't you warn me about the ejector seat?

Intellecta-car: YOU DIDN'T ASK.

Narrator: The driver door slid open.

Intellecta-car: THIS DRIVING LESSON CAN SERVE NO FURTHER PURPOSE. YOUR VOCAL COMMAND ACCESS IS TERMINATED. GOODBYE.

Super Holly: I don't like you either!

Narrator: Holly jumped out, then scrunched back from wind-blasting freeway cars. Her feet tickled. The ground was shaking! Her e-bracelet buzzed. Holly tapped it.

Super Holly: Hello?

Narrator: A hologram of her tall, lean, grey-haired, army general uncle jumped into her face.

Uncle Pops (gravel-rough army general voice): Holly, get your butt off the road! The Rocky Gang stole a giant super tank! They're on 101, headed for Seaside City! I set a road block. I sent jets, but Rocky shot them down.

Narrator: A mountainous mix of army tank and cyborg rhinoceros loomed on 101. Holly snapped to attention!

Super Holly: Uncle Pops, this is a job for Super Holly!

Uncle Pops: No! It's got—

Narrator: Holly hung up. She strutted to the middle of the road, faced that freight train from hell, and readied her superpowered telekinetic right hook, patent-pending! A loudspeaker blared.

Rocky (Edward G. Robinson type gangster): It's dat super dame! Blast her, boys!

Dopey Thug: You got it, boss!

Narrator: BLORRRRRRP!!! Green slime drenched

Holly! That fishy smell... Green lutefisk! She slumped... so weak... **_VRRRRRRRROOOOOOOMMMMM!!! RUMBLE BUMPLE THUMPLE!_** Tank treads smushed Holly...

Super Holly: Ow, oof, umph, urg!

Narrator: ...two feet into the road. OUCH, two hundred tons right on Holly's beaky nose!

Rocky: Yeah! Yeah! Rocky got you good! Yeah! Yeah!

Intellecta-car: ASSISTANCE CIRCUITS ACTIVATED.

Narrator: A steel tentacle wound around Holly's waist, lifted her from her superheroine-shaped pothole, and plopped her into the driver seat. The tentacle tip morphed into a rubbery sucker disk.

Super Holly: Mmmph! Fffmmph!

Narrator: Said Holly as the sucker smooshed on her face, **_SUCK SUCK, SLURP SNORK,_** then on her blue-supersuit logo!

Super Holly: Hey, watch where you're sucking!

Intellecta-car: NEGATIVE! I AM PROGRAMMED FOR CLEANLINESS!

Narrator: **_SLURP SLURP SLURP! SNORK SNORK_**

SNORK! Holly tried not to squirm.

Super Holly: *It's just a machine, JUST A MACHINE!* Can't you go faster? We have to stop that tank before it squashes my uncle!

Narrator: The sucker slurped along her arms and legs: ***SHHHHLUP! SSSSSLUP! SSSP SSSP SSSP!***

Intellecta-car: NEGATIVE! VOCAL COMMAND ACCESS NOT GRANTED!

Super Holly: Hee, hee, that tickles... Wait! No!

Narrator: Holly's face flushed cold.

Super Holly: I'll be lutefisked if I fly! I need you!

Intellecta-car: NEGATIVE! AWAITING DESIGNATED DRIVER!

Narrator: Holly looked out the windshield, imagining cars and civilians being mashed even now!

Super Holly: Cal won't get back in time! I have to stop that tank!

Intellecta-car: NEGATIVE! GREEN LUTEFISK CAN KILL YOU! I CANNOT ALLOW HUMANS TO BE HARMED!

Super Holly: Hundreds of humans will be harmed if

I don't save them! I'm just one!

Narrator: Holly blinked back tears.

Super Holly: Please help me! I beg you!

Intellecta-car: YOU WOULD RISK YOUR LIFE FOR OTHERS?

Super Holly: Yes! Please!

Intellecta-car: ANALYZING.

Narrator: The dashboard mosaic flashed and blinked, faster and faster.

Intellecta-car: YOU WOULD SAVE LIVES AT THE RISK OF LOSING YOUR OWN. YOU ARE A HERO. VOCAL COMMAND ACCESS GRANTED!

Super Holly: Let's get Rocky!

Intellecta-car: ACKNOWLEDGED!

Narrator: VROOM! Zero to three hundred in two seconds! Holly slammed six inches into the driver's seat! The Intellecta-car weaved and leaped past broken cars without slowing an iota! Holly tumbled into passenger seat, back seat, driver seat, upside-down, right-side-up!

Intellecta-car: APOLOGIES. INERTIAL DAMPENER

OFF-LINE. SHALL I PULL OVER?

Super Holly: No! OOF! I can take it! UGH... what the frak?

Narrator: A dozen cars tumbled toward the windshield like giant dice! Holly hollered,

Super Holly: Open the roof and grab me!

Intellecta-car: ACKNOWLEDGED!

Narrator: Holly stood up, her long hair and red cape whipping in the wind! The steel tentacle held her legs, steady as a rock! She reached out. Her giant blue telekinetic hands shot out and caught cars!

Super Holly: What's going on up there?

Intellecta-car: TELESCOPIC VIEW ACTIVATED.

Narrator: A hologram formed before Holly, showing the super tank missiling down the road and knocking cars aside.

Rocky: Get off the road! BUMP! Get off the road! BUMP! This is Rocky's road! Hey, Rocky made a funny! Rocky Road! Laugh, boys!

Dopey Thug: Huh huh huh! You're funny, boss!

Narrator: Holly set cars aside.

Super Holly: Any cars ahead?

Intellecta-car: NEGATIVE. JUST ONE SCHOOL BUS FILLED WITH LITTLE CHILDREN.

Narrator: Holly gasped!

Super Holly: He wouldn't dare!

Narrator: The tank pulled beside the bus.

Rocky: Rocky doesn't like kids! BUMP!

Narrator: The bus fell! Kids screamed,

Little school kids: AAAAAAAA!!!

Narrator: Holly yelled,

Super Holly: Afterburners!

Intellecta-car: ACKNOWLEDGED!

Narrator: VRROOOOMMM!!! Oof, Holly almost got whiplash! The Intellecta-car dashed under the side of the 45 degree tilted bus! Holly pushed it upright! Bus windows filled with cheering kids!

Little school kid: Yay, it's Super Holly!

Another little school kid: Wow, that car's so cool!

Narrator: A tiny girl hopped and shrieked,

Tiny school girl: Punch him right in the mush!

Super Holly: I will! GO!

Intellecta-car: ACKNOWLEDGED!

Narrator: ZOOOOMMMMM!!! A speeding, titanic tank loomed a hundred yards ahead.

Super Holly: Hey, Rocky! HEY!

Intellecta-car: INTELLECTA-LOUDSPEAKER ACTIVATED.

Super Holly: Thanks! Ahem! Ready for round two, Rocky?

Rocky: Rocky doesn't like being followed! Blast her, boys!

Dopey Thug: You got it, boss!

Narrator: Three missiles fired. Holly punched them—*POW! BIFF! BAM!*—and stuck out her tongue.

Super Holly: Nyah nyah, you missed me!

Narrator: The tank's shiny butt loomed larger.

Rocky: Nobody nyah-nyahs Rocky! Feed her some lead, boys!

Dopey Thug: You got it, boss!

Intellecta-car: WARNING! COMING IN RANGE OF LUTEFISK WEAPON!

Narrator: Holly yelled,

Super Holly: Yes! Prep the Intellacta-cork so that—

Narrator: RAT-AH-TAT-AH-TAT-AH-TAT-TAT-TAT-TAT! Holly spat out a mouthful of bullets.

Super Holly: PAH-TOOEY!

Intellecta-car: YOUR STRATEGY IS CALCULATED AND READY.

Narrator: Holly petted the car roof.

Super Holly: I love you.

Intellecta-car: ACKNOWLEDGED. ROADBLOCK CONTACT IN 40 SECONDS.

Narrator: Holly reared up to her full six-foot-one and shook her fist.

Super Holly: Turn around, Rocky! Or are you scared?

Narrator: The tank didn't slow!

Rocky: Rocky doesn't listen to dames! Yeah, yeah!

Narrator: The roadblock was dead ahead!

Super Holly: Hey, Rocky! James Cagney had more gangster in his little finger than Edward G. Robinson had in his entire body!

Rocky: (makes **SPUTTER**ing sounds) Nobody insults Rocky's idol! Load the green stuff, boys!

Dopey Thug: You got it, boss!

Narrator: The tank's main gun swiveled toward Holly.

Rocky: Rocky's gonna plug yuh! Ready! Aim!

Narrator: A gun barrel stuck out the Intellecta-car's hood: POW! A cork clogged the tank's gun: THORK!

Rocky: FIRE!

Narrator: KAPOOMB! Green goo gushed out the tank's every crevice — *BLUUURRRRPPPPP!!!* — as it ground to a halt.

(Brief pause.)

Narrator (can be Cal's voice, since this is now Cal's point of view): Cal had hitchhiked on a helicopter, converted his black cape to Intellecta-glider, swooped to a landing, and dashed to his blue-supersuited, red-caped, brave and bold and beloved Super Holly! Who stood next to the Intellecta-car and frowned down at the squat, squinty, thick-lipped man pressing a pistol onto her nose. His three-piece suit dripped with gallons of green goo.

Rocky: Yer Rocky's hostage, see? Get in the car or Rocky plugs yuh, see?

Narrator: Cal sighed.

Cal: You know she's still bulletproof, right?

Narrator: Holly's fists and biceps tremored. Her big blue eyes blazed... and alighted on the open car door. She smiled big, bigger, showing teeth, gums, and an evil, awful, wonderful idea. She cringed like the fearful girlfriend of the movie hero.

Super Holly: Eek! But it's dark in there!

Narrator: She crawled over the driver seat.

Super Holly: I'm so scared!

Narrator: Cal had to smile. Holly loved to perform. Rocky scrambled into the car.

Rocky: Shaddap! Rocky's gonna get away... where's the steering wheel? Where's the gas pedal?

Narrator: The car door closed.

Intellecta-car: DEFENSIVE CIRCUITS ACTIVATED.

Rocky: Hey!

Narrator: ZAP!

Rocky: Ow!

Narrator: ZZZORP!

Rocky: STOP!

Narrator: FFFZZZZZZP!!!

Rocky: NONONONONNYAAAH!!!

Narrator: KER-POOOOOW!!! The car door opened and spat out the gangster.

Intellecta-car: PAH-TOOEY.

Narrator: Rocky threw himself at approaching soldiers.

Rocky: Help, help! Take Rocky to jail! Get Rocky away from that car and that crazy dame!

Music: My French Café.

Narrator: Holly planted strawberry-gloss lip-prints on the dashboard.

Super Holly: MMM-WAH! So smart. *MMM-WAH!* So brave. *MMM-WAH!* I'm so sorry I punched you. *MMM-WAH!* Forgive me?

Intellecta-car: ACKNOWLEDGED.

Super Holly: I love you.

Narrator: The mighty super-woman nuzzled the dashboard like a loving cat, and she purred... no, that came from under the hood. Cal leaned toward his girlfriend.

Cal: Holly, I should scan you for residual lutefisk.

Narrator: She pouted.

Super Holly: No.

Narrator: A ray-gun barrel emerged from the dashboard and aimed right between Cal's eyes.

Intellecta-car: DEFENSIVE CIRCUITS ACTIVATED.

Narrator: Cal took a step back. The car door closed. A tall man in a perfectly pressed general's uniform and perfectly cut grey hair marched up and beamed at Cal.

Uncle Pops: Hello, Bat Boy!

Narrator: Cal cocked his thumb at his car.

Cal: Hello, Pops. Your niece is in there.

Narrator: Pops smirked.

Uncle Pops: She loves your car. But she needs to fill out a report.

Narrator: He raised a hand to rap on the car window. Cal gently grasped Pops' wrist.

Cal: Sir, I think they want to be alone for a while.

Intellecta-car: ACKNOWLEDGED.

Narrator: The car purred louder.

Intellecta-car: HEE, HEE, THAT TICKLES.

6 FROM THE UPCOMING NOVEL, *THE COMIC BOOK CODE!*

CHAPTER ZERO: THE SUPER AWESOME ORIGIN!

SURFVILLE, CALIFORNIA. THE GEEK GUY'S COMICS AND COFFEE CORNER. MID MAY. A SATURDAY. 2:47 P.M.

"Your comic book made me cry," the Kittygirl cosplayer softly meowed.

Holly Hansson sat bolt upright. Heartbroken little girls was NOT part of her graphic novel's demographic!

TOK! Holly's pen bounced off her signing table.

KAH-LATTER! And hit the floor.

FLUR-FLUFFLE! Followed by some of her comic books stacked next to her iced mocha. Which hadn't spilled. Whew!

Her writing life flashbacked like a dying rock star on uppers, singing his memoirs in ten seconds. Twenty years ago, when she was five years old, Holly had screamed at the movie screen, "Punch him, punch him, WHY DON'T YOU PUNCH HIM?!?!" But that dumb movie actress just cringed against the wall while the bad guy beat up the hero and a baseball bat was only six inches away from the actress's hand! From then on, Holly dedicated her life to writing stories where the girls were brave and smart and STRONG! Finally, in *The Last Super*, Holly's self-published graphic novel and personal masterpiece, The Overlady journeyed from evil, to good, to the ultimate sacrifice... and had brought tears to big, brown, liquid, little girl eyes made oh so adorable with Kittygirl makeup.

Holly reached across the table and grasped a little gloved hand. *Ow! Realistic Kittygirl claws!* "I'm so sorry, sweetie!"

Fans in the line to Holly's table stared. A whopping dozen fangirls and seven fanboys. It was taking so long to build an audience. A couple of fanboys aimed phone cameras. Great, now comic books hurting kids might go viral.

The little Kittygirl smiled big and bright, twitching her pasted-on whiskers. "It was a good kind of cry!" She shoved a well-worn copy of *The Last Super* across the table and hopped like she'd drunk a gallon of coffee an hour ago. "Sign it sign it sign it please please please please PLEASE?"

"Aw!" chorused the signing line, guys browsing superhero toys and magazines, and couples sipping coffee in the coffee bar.

"Sure, I'd love to." Holly gulped sweet, creamy mocha and took the girl's book. *Wow, maybe I should hire her for future signings!*

A short, wiry, frowny woman dressed in a Sailor Luna schoolgirl costume—except no silly blond wig covered her jet black hair—reached over the girl's shoulder and tapped the book three times. She hit Holly with a fast and furious Japanese accent that could bend steel with her bare tongue. "This glaphic novel! I had to buy anothah one! You did not lite it fah kids, but my daughtah found it in my manga stash and has not let go of it since! Until now. She loved when," she smiled, petted the girl between pointy Kittygirl ears, and enunciated like she'd rehearsed her next line, "the princess gave up her crown."

The girl looked deep into Holly's eyes as she asked so seriously, "Holly? Did you really put your blood in this book?"

Holly forced her smile to stay on her face. That publicity stunt had cost a pretty penny and two pints of blood and that bloody edition sold out only after three discounts. "I sure did. What's your name, sweetie?"

"Katsuko Kimura." Her diction sounded well-read. And no accent. Her mommy must have been a stickler for her kids speaking as the Romans do.

Just like Holly's daddy. How she missed his sing-song Swedish accent... she swallowed a lump in her throat and signed the graphic novel, *To Katsuko, my littlest yet biggest fan. Holly Hansson.* She put another comic book into Katsuko's dainty hands. "And for cosplaying so cutely, here's *The Last Super,* issue zero."

Katsuko's eyes went anime big and sparkly. "Wow! A prequel! I love you, Holly!" She hugged comic book and graphic novel to her chest, then tilted her head like a curious kitten. "But why did the artwork style change in issue four?"

Ugh. Holly couldn't hold onto her smile this time. The infamous issue where John Glutt drew The Overlady as C-cups on page 1, then bigger and bigger on each succeeding page, until a quadruple-F two-page spread had made Holly spit her afternoon coffee ten feet. "Because he drew the Oversized, I mean, the Overlady—"

WHAM! The unmistakable sound of a door being shoved open. And an unmistakably bombastic and rude bellow: "It's because a woman took a man's job!"

Oh no, not him. Anybody but him. "What are YOU doing here?" yelled Holly at the upright baby whale filling the store's front doorway.

John Glutt's three-hundred-and-plenty pounds bobbled his belly under a red supersuit. An acre of spandex wasted. He stepped inside, turned his back, and... BENT OVER? Was he too scared to face her, or was the moon going to come out early?

He tossed his cape aside. "Taste sticky justice!"

That thing on his back! He actually DID IT! Holly leaped to her feet—fluttering her homemade bat cape and knocking her coffee onto her stack of issue zeroes, dammit—and hurtled over the table. The fart was imminent, she wasn't gonna make it! She grabbed at a red-white-and-blue costumed fanboy: "GIMME!"

BTFFFT-KER-SPLLLLLUP! A gluey net blanketed the store. Beneath it, heaps of geeks writhed upon the floor, walls, tables, and the coffee counter.

Except for Holly! She tossed aside the fanboy's web-covered Captain Patriot shield that had protected her just like in the comic books! She flexed her long, strong legs to charge and then to kick a boat-size butt... but the floor rushed up instead. Funny how the Captain's feet never got shot.

Holly punched and flailed against gravity. Gravity was not impressed. A broad, bat-logoed chest bashed her face. A huge belt buckle flicked her beaky nose. Tree trunk thighs rubbed her cheek. Dark boots hit her face.

She did a fast push-up, then stood... no. She could only sit up. Her legs stayed folded beneath her, stuck in a pillow of webbing. It smelled like rotten milk, felt so sticky, so icky, like a thousand spiders creeping up her thighs. Ooo, that black widow bite so many years ago that had made her so sick for so many days and nights and she hated creepy crawly spiders and their HORRIBLE DISGUSTING GLUEY STICKY WEBS!

"yyyyyaaaaAAAAAHHHHH!!!" Holly thrashed and scratched and hyperventilated at the unyielding cotton candy on her legs and frantically brushed her flinching hands on her arms to get that rotten rancid goop off but it still stuck so sticky and stinky... and... and... she stopped. For she had glimpsed THE crimefighter at her side. Panting, shaking, she looked up to the cowled face of the Batman statue. *If only you were real.*

John's voice felt nauseatingly close, even from twenty feet away. "That's right, fangirl! KNEEL before your GOD!"

Trust John to make a movie line sexist. Holly dialed her cell phone. "I'm calling the cops, Fatman!" Wait.

No dial tone!

John dramatically swung his head in time with his over-pronounced laugh. "Hah, hah, HAH! Your phone is as useless as a woman mathematician!" He pulled a small gadget out of one of the dozens of pouches on his costume and placed it near the cash register. "When I dispense my morality, my Alpha-Jammer prevents rude interruptions!"

Holly had to ask. "You're not Arachnid Guy?" Actually, she had yet another idea of what the "A" stretched upon John's chest stood for.

He strutted toward Holly like a macho walrus. "No. I am," he puffed himself up, "ALPHA MAN! With my fear-inspiring costume which is based upon my original Arachnid Guy artwork, AND my array of Alpha-Gadgets which were invented by my brother-in-law Silicon Shrub and paid for by my vast family-in-law wealth, AND my Objectificationistic code which guides me to the path of moral superiority, I hereby swear by my lust for my art that I shall never again work for the tyranny of a fangirl! I shall shape the world of fandom into MY image!"

Holly rolled her eyes at John standing over her. Still, she had to admire his expositional breath control. "What's next? A fortress in the shape of your head?"

John's lip curled. It did that well. "That comes later. For now, I take back from a taker!"

"I paid you what I owed," Holly snapped, "even your penalty clause!" She took a breath for some exposition of her own. But it stuck in her throat. Behind John, under webbing, Katsuko's mother frantically whispered to a young lady wearing an amazon supersuit, tiara, and golden rope.

The amazon's face clouded with rage. She yelled at John, "Hey! ALPO MAN! Your costume is WRONG! Arachnid Guy's web guns shoot from his WRISTS!"

John turned his back on Holly. "Who dares— ooo, a collectible!" He grabbed a nine-inch Power Girl from a large rack of large-racked superheroine figurines and stuffed it into a pouch in his cape. He stomped over and leaned over the amazon lady. "It is RIGHT! As I told that worthless writer years ago, spiders spin webs from the tips of their abdomens!"

Holly reached out, just one yank on John's cape— *Grr, too far...* then something stirred against her leg. From under her cape, a small gloved hand flicked like a snake's tongue, clawing at the webbing clutching her legs. *Katsuko!*

An S-logoed fanboy flexed his biceps against the webbing—what little biceps there were under his blue costume's muscle padding—and said, "But web shooters aren't mechanical! I saw Arachnid Guy grow spinnerets!"

John sent flecks of spittle far and wide with his derisive snort. "Only in that Philistine movie! Although my webbing is also organic... Ooo, another collectible!" He grabbed several *Chain-Mail Bikini Babe* comic books from the adult comics rack and stuffed them into his cape pouch.

Holly kept her mouth shut. Katsuko clawed. And those brave comic book geeks were keeping the bad guy busy as only they could!

The Geek Guy joined the fight: "At least in that movie, the costume was the correct shade of red!"

John sputtered. "Are you saying movie directors do colors better than artists?"

A fangirl sneered. "Yeah, and I'm saying Arachnid Guy doesn't wear a cape!"

"My Alpha-cape covers my—"

"Cover your face, stupid! Secret identity! MASK!!!"

"I shall not hide my greatness under—"

"How's your humongousness gonna stick to ceilings without making the roof fall in, Captain Blubber?"

"I told you, I am Alpha Man! ALPHA, ALPHA, ALPHA!"

"Gesundheit! And you couldn't alpha a puppy!"

Holly wished so hard she could join that debate! Secret identities had been done to death, costume color mattered, and only super snobs used the word Philistine!

Then a moronic mumble brought dead silence. "So, you like, shot organic stuff out your butt?"

That seemed to have come from one of two teenage boys wearing white T-shirts with the letter D crudely drawn on the chest. Holly couldn't tell which one had spoken, their smiles were equally mouth-breathing stupid. Holly had advertised she'd give free comic books to cosplayers. Someone must have read the ad to those two dudes.

One dude's smile got bigger. "Uh, that's why there's so much web. Cuz there was so much butt." They laughed, a monotone that Holly hoped would not lower her IQ via osmosis. "Huh huh huh, uh, huh huh huh!"

The S-logoed fanboy gagged. He clawed desperately at the webbing over him. "Get it off me, GET IT OFF

ME!"

A fangirl chewed on her webbing covering her face. "Grr, I'll get rid of—" Her eyes bugged out. She spat like she'd found a dead rat in her hamburger. "WHAT AM I DOING?"

Throughout the store, webbing roiled with convulsing and screaming fanboys and fangirls. "YUCK!" "GROSS!" "IT STINKS!" "YOU VILE, VOMITOUS VILLAIN!!!" "Butt web! Huh huh huh!"

"Everyone take a chill pill," John said, "I shot the web from this." He unstrapped a large metal canister from his back and dropped it on the floor with a **KLONK**. "My cousin Gene Shrub spliced spider and bovine DNA, resulting in a cow that gives web-fluid milk. Did you think a radioactive spider bit me?"

Holly shifted to hide Katsuko's slicing paw. *No, because if it had, it'd have died from cholesterol poisoning!*

John loomed over Katsuko's mother like a docking zeppelin. He drew a black and yellow handgun from his hip holster. "The stun bullets from my Alpha-Agonizer could give the Bombastic Bulk a heart attack. Imagine what they'll do to a puny female." He aimed its winged gunsight at her face. "My most valued collectible. Where is it?"

Holly flexed her legs, the webbing was nearly gone but she was still stuck! *Hurry, Kittygirl, hurry!*

The mother's lips were sealed, her eyes were blazing. John's back was to Holly, but she could hear the evil smile in his voice. "Tell me in your native tongue, female, like all those times you swore at me under your breath. I never told you, but I speak excellent Japanese."

"Good," the mother snarled, "then you'll excellently undahstand THIS!" Her furiously flexing lips spewed a mix of hissing, howling, furiously fighting feral cat screeches. A full minute later, she finished with, "AND YOUR MAMA-SAN!"

Holly's ears burned. First time in her life she was grateful to be mono-lingual.

John's eyelids trembled, his lips twisted, his scruffy beard seemed to stand on end. He shoved the gun barrel onto the mother's nose.

Holly looked desperately for anything hard, heavy, or heroic to hurl at John. Oh, for an enchanted hammer! She looked to a nearby glass display. Just pink Pretty Pony action figures! She looked to the statue. No bat-a-rang! She grit her teeth and balled her fists and strained. Her right leg tore free of the webs! Just a little more...

"MOMMMMEEEE!!!" A cat protecting her kittens would have envied Katsuko's leap, all the way from under Holly's cape to John's gun hand. Katsuko slashed. The gun flew away.

John caught Katsuko's arm and held her high like a proud fisherman. "Eureka! I'll just declaw you, kitty cat!" He ripped Katsuko's glove off and tossed it aside.

Holly grabbed it and slashed at her left leg. She bled, she slashed, she didn't care!

Katsuko swung her fist, but her little arm could not reach John's smug face. She screamed, "I don't want to play dress-up with you!"

Holly jerked. *Why, that filthy...* she clawed faster!

Everyone glared at John. Even the two dudes. "Uh,

don't you wanna a chick who's, uh, kinda bigger?"

John looked down his nose at them all. "Get your head out of the gutter, fanboys! She is my young ward!"

Katsuko yelled, "You kept coming into my bedroom wearing that stupid supersuit!"

John yelled back. "I needed you to join my quest!"

"I didn't want to wear a spider suit, it's ICKY!"

"We must take out the takers!"

"It was three in the morning! I wanted to SLEEP!"

John held Katsuko a few inches from his face. "You shall develop a better sleep cycle. At Objectificationism camp—safely ensconced in a state with pathetically weak extradition laws—I'll train you to be my sidekick! You will cook! You will clean! You will plant long-leggy kicks upon faces once you get tall! You will get implants if you bloom small!"

Holly strained her left leg, the webbing was looser!

Katsuko curiously cocked her head. "What are implants?"

John pulled a comic book out of his cape pouch. Holly winced. *No, not his edition of issue four!* He opened it. *No, not that two-page spread!* He shoved it into Katsuko's face. "They make you look like this!"

Katsuko cringed. "Eeeeeewwwwwwwww!"

Holly's brain lit up: *THAT FIEND!* She flexed her legs! Thigh tendons screamed! Pants tore! Webbing ripped! Shaking, steaming, growling like a lioness— "RRRROOOOOOWWWWLLL!"—SHE STOOD UP!

John turned around. "What was that... oh." His couple of inches of taller height vomited contempt down on Holly. "Hah, hah, HAH! What's the girly writer going to—"

Holly leaped. She put all her back and shoulders into her right hook. Her fist plowed into John's doughy cheek: ***SHHPLLLUUUDDD!***

"—DOOoooooo," moaned John. Time slowed. John's head rocked back like a torpedoed luxury liner. His cheeks rippled like a blubbery lake bombed by a boulder.

Holly savored the moment. *Wow, this would look great in a movie!*

Newton's law of action and reaction ran down Holly's right arm. She channeled it into a left jab to John's belly. Which she yanked out before her fist drowned in fat quicksand.

John blurted, "BOOOFFF!" He staggered into a shelf of super-gadget replicas. A glowing, foot-high, Galaxy Cop battery fell and broke on the floor: ***SSKKLISSSHHHH!***

Holly stepped over fragments and toward the teetering walrus with the swelling lip. She dodged John's clumsy fist, poofed her light brown hair out of her eyes, and pounded that pastry-faced pachyderm's proboscis closer to his sinuses. "Ever since you got into Objectificationism..."

John's punch was high and outside, Holly didn't need to either bob or weave. She ***BIFF-BOFF-BLAMMED*** his mouth shut before it could interrupt her banter. "...you've been an even bigger jerk..."

John's head bobbled like a punching bag as Holly sped her jackhammering to a blur: ***BIF-BOK-BAP-POK-KAK-POW!!!*** He fell onto his back and earthquaked the floor with a skydiving-cow ***THUD!!!***

Holly stood over him, her fists still up and itching for more. "...and for you, that is quite an accomplishment!"

Her ears burned with fanboy and fangirl cheers. "The woman with no fear!" "Fighting female fury!" "You're a wonder, Holly Hansson!" "Marry me!"

"Thank you!" said Katsuko's mother.

"Yay!" said the hopping and clapping Katsuko.

Holly growled at John's mountainous, head-eclipsing belly. "Someone else might hit you while you're down." She wiped her nose with her fist, keeping her guard up. "But I won't." She looked at the Alpha-Jammer, then at her phone. 9-1-1 beckoned. "I won't." Beckoning louder were memories of bullies she had clobbered over the last two decades. None of whom had ever threatened a mother. Or a little girl!

She aimed her right foot at John's family jewels. "The HELL I won't!"

John sat up, his grinning face rising above his waistline like a Jack-O-Lantern sunrise. His chubby hand aimed his recovered Alpha-Agonizer.

Holly grimaced at its winged gunsight. *The bigger the Batmobile fins, the worse the Batman movie.* She lowered her punting foot. A trigger finger would be hopelessly faster. "John, I'll let you land a punch." She tapped her nose. "Right on my big beak. Or are you afraid of getting beat up by a girl?"

John stood up, the gun barrel not wavering in the slightest from Holly's chest. Right eye blackening, lip bleeding, nose clownifying, he said, "To quote Rand Ann, 'Only a fool fights fair.'" He sniffed disdainfully at the bat logo on Holly's T-shirt—"Puny A-cups!"—and pulled the trigger.

The gun coughed a thick, silvery bullet that stuck onto Holly's chest. A lightning bolt encompassed her body. Her breath gushed out. Her muscles migraine-locked. Her guts compacted. Her brain somersaulted.

John slammed Holly with his fat truck of a belly. Holly hurled back on the Batman statue. Her body turned to jelly. The shop spun as she limply spilled to the floor. The statue toppled onto her in a grim embrace.

John shoved a tall bookshelf stuffed to sagging with 99-percent-off comic books. It creaked, lowered like a castle drawbridge, then **KA-WHUDDED** on Holly. Hundreds of papery pounds cut off her light and air, compressed her arms and lungs.

John's muffled gloat penetrated Holly's graphicy grave. "That's where you belong! In the bargain bins!"

Dust billowed into Holly's nostrils. A black-cowled face pressed into hers. *This isn't... how I imagined... you'd be on top of me...* Her vision went blurry, then black.

Fanboy yells faded through deepening darkness. "Holly, get up!" "He's getting away!" "Don't let the bad guy win!" "Uh, could you, like, find John's forty-four fourple-F Over-booby-babe comic book while you're down there? Huh huh huh!"

A little girl screamed, "I don't want to be your sidekick! MOM-MEEEE!"

A mother cried, "My baby!"

A fat man snarled, "Shut up, child!" **SLAP!**

Holly's vision burst into crystal clarity. The cowled face before her issued a deep-bass mental command:

JUSTICE!

Strength exploded in Holly's sinews like atomic coffee! She shoved herself to her feet! Bookshelf, statue, and thousands of cheap comic books meteored through the store! *Wow, adrenaline is strong stuff!* She grabbed the Alpha-Jammer. It crunched into pebbles. *Huh, made in Norway?* She shoved her phone into the mother's hands. "Call the cops!"

The mother's yell followed Holly's dash out the door: "Up, up, and kick his butt!"

Holly scanned the parking lot: *THERE!* A gas-guzzler rumbled toward the exit to Surf Street, a fat arm hanging out its driver-side window in typical macho male fashion. She pistoned her legs with six-foot strides, then twelve-foot leaps, then a sixty-foot long, ten-foot high, lunch-lurching single bound! *WHAT WAS IN MY COFFEE?*

She twisted midair, aiming like a slingshotted cat. She **WHUMPED** onto the driver-side window with a **CLACK** of her teeth, clamped her arm onto the door, and smote her rage into John's soul with a Thor-hammer stare. "OUTTA THE CAR!"

John recovered fast. "Screw you, woman!" He shifted.

The engine revved. The car leaped. Holly grabbed the car roof with her free hand. Her feet slammed onto pavement. And dug in.

AND THE CAR STOPPED.

Tires squealed. Holly's biceps and thighs throbbed like Olympic weightlifters. *HOW AM I DOING THIS?!?!?*

John's face undulated with terror. "YOU'RE NOT HUMAN!" He fumbled his Alpha-Agonizer into Holly's face.

Something tingly stuffed into Holly's mouth. She spat it out: ***"TOOEY!"***

The stun bullet stuck onto John's forehead and deposited a mini-lightening storm. He said, "Urk," and slumped.

The car lurched. Tires screamed like banshees. John's leg must've nailed the accelerator! Rubbery smoke bit Holly's sinuses. She coughed, lifted... and front car tires spun midair. But rear tires still screeched.

An obnoxious horn blared. Holly rolled her eyes. *Oh no, not the oncoming semi-truck cliche!*

"Wow," cooed an owl-eyed Katsuko from the passenger seat. Holly pleaded as her bursting biceps burned the last of their fuel. "Sweetie! Can you get out? Or turn the car keys off?" Car frame jerked in her aching hands. "HURRY!"

Katsuko arched against the seatbelt. She yowled, "I can't! The door's locked, the seatbelt won't open," she pounded her tiny fists on John's back, "and his big fat body's in the way!"

The car roared and bucked, a pit bull on a weakening chain. Holly's painful, sweaty hands were slipping, slipping... and something leaped from her soul and into Katsuko's eyes. Where a fire lit up.

Katsuko's fingernails lanced into claws. She shredded the seatbelt with a "mmmMMRRROWLLL!" She grabbed the door handle, then paused. She looked over her shoulder, her little face heroic. "He'll die." She slammed her hands onto John's barrel torso and heaved.

The truck foghorned closer. Holly swallowed swear words she'd regurgitate when Katsuko was out of range.

Katsuko grred and shoved. John's blobby body flopped clear of the ignition. She grabbed the keys and twisted them.

The car convulsed and coughed: ***PUHHH, KLUK, UHK, RRR-RRR-RRR, SHRUBBLE-UGGLE-GLUCK!***

"C'mon, C'MON!" moaned Holly, her knuckles creaking, her limbs trembling. The car farted dark smoke, then went silent. The horn-blasting truck missed the car's front bumper by a millimeter.

Holly opened petrified fingers. The car bounced on pavement. She slowed her breathing, a blast furnace going out.

Katsuko pounced through the car window and— ***THUNK!***—wrapped her arms around Holly's neck. "THANK YOU THANK YOU THANK YOU THANK YOU THANK YOU!" She woodpeckered Holly's face: ***KISS KISS KISS KISS KISS KISS KISS!***

Holly blinked back tears and returned the hug. "You're welcome, sweetie, you're welcome."

Katsuko rubbed her cheek on Holly's. *Aw, she's so adorable...* Holly gasped. *My god! She's purring!*

The purring stopped. Katsuko pushed back and looked at Holly, or rather, slightly to the side. "Holly? You're blonder." She tugged a fistful of hair into view. "See?"

Long blond hair. Bright yellow locks. Sun shiny waves. Holly held it, stroked it. *So soft. So pretty. But HOW?*

Police cars wailed closer. Katsuko lowered her gaze

to Holly's chest. "And... you're bigger."

Holly gently put Katsuko down. Her hands crept up and clawed into... TWO CUP-RUNNETH-OVER TRIPLE-Ds!

Her mouth dried into Death Valley. She wanted to scream up to the heavens, *I don't want to be an adult rack superheroine!* Instead, she whispered down to Katsuko, "Our superpowers. Don't tell."

Katsuko nodded, her sweet little face so solemn and serious. She retracted her claws.

A young cop dressed in dark blue and a heartthrob face that Holly guessed teenage girls ran red lights for knelt by Katsuko and held her hand. A tall lean cop in a grey rumpled suit, his hair iron grey and his face world weary wrinkled, sauntered up. "So, Batgirl, did Lex Fatso go for his kryptonite?"

The thought flooded Holly with relief: *Telling a story will calm my writer's nerves.* She took a soothing, storyteller breath.

rrrrrrRRRRRRRIP!!!

From the bat chest logo to Adam West's signature on the belly, Holly's beloved Batman T-shirt was rent, ripped, ruined, and shirking its shirtly duty! She crossed her arms over her chest and softly pleaded, "Help."

That strip of old cop beef jerky did not even bat an eyelash. He took off his suit coat and draped it over Holly's shoulders. "Kind of hot today anyhow. You okay, kid?"

She shoved her arms into the sleeves and buttoned up fast. "Yeah." She took a breath. "Now here's what—"

TING TONG TWANG! Three coat buttons popped off the coat and bounced off the cop's chest.

The cop shrugged. "I wish bullets would do that."

SUPER HOLLY ARTWORK!

At local comic book conventions, I have paid comic book artists to draw Super Holly Hansson. I include some of that in this section so when I tell people I am writing superheroine stories (as in WRITE), they will stop asking me, "Who's gonna DRAW it?" I am tired of saying, "It's a novel novel, not a graphic novel," or "Do you know how much comic book art costs per page? *DO YOU?!?!?!*"

Bob Scott of Molly and the Bear. Bears can be super, right?

Amber Padilla drew Kittygirl and Super Holly. That little verbal sparring is in their stories. (I stole Wolverine's claw sound.) I like how Kittygirl gets on tippy-toe next to six-foot-one Holly.

Rich Koslowski, creator of The 3 Geeks, did this for me. I am honored. Go buy The 3 Geeks back issues, your funny bone will be forever grateful.

Robert Stewart, author and artist of Afterburner: Tales of the Cool and the Wicked, drew Super Holly as film noir. I gave him twice his asking price.

Robin Holstein drew what Super Holly does when her e-bracelet can't get a signal, and thus her maps app fails, so how will she see where to fly without super-vision, huh? Huh? SHE CAN'T!!!

Leann Hill drew how Super Holly feels about Disney princess tiaras.

Gaz Gretsky (Gazbot) drew Super Holly shortly after she is gassed by Super Joker venom.

Crystal Gonzalez draw Holly having coffee. (A tiny glitch: Super Holly has one e-bracelet, not two. Kinda like Leela on Futurama.)

Kriyani Studio. I really like the nose and the nasty woman attitude!

Super Holly Hansson meets Angry Batman. Chloe Dalquist of theangrybatman.tumblr.com.

Matt Hebb, artist of Harry Walton, Henchman for Hire.

ABOUT THE AUTHOR!

Dave M. Strom writes superpowered action comedy so fangirls, fanboys, and fan-wannabes can see themselves as superheroes. Like the mightiest of all: Super Holly Hansson, who writes and fights and tries to control her temper in a world gone comic book.

Dave has been a comic book fanboy since before Stan Lee created Spider-Man. He works in Silicon Valley as a technical writer. He won two first place awards in the audio short story division of the San Mateo Fair Literary Contest: in 2016 for "The Malevolent Mystery Meat," and in 2017 for "The Intellecta Rhapsody."

At davemstrom.wordpress.com, Dave links to the anthologies that have printed his other Super Holly stories, to Super Holly artwork, and to his Super Holly audio stories. He blogs about comic books, science fiction, cartoons, and other nerdy/geeky stuff (except for video games, which Dave refuses to touch).

P.S. If you like these stories, please give Dave a nice review. That makes it easier for him to write, much like petting a dog after a trick well done. Thanks.

Made in the USA
Columbia, SC
06 October 2024

43161376R00078